Delusional Dreams

TRUTH OF DELUSIONS
BOOK ONE

MARIA TANDY

Connor thank you !

Maria ♡
Tandy

María Tandy

Delusional Dreams

María Tandy

www.mariatandyauthor.com

Cover Design: Eunice Fernandez

Editing by Jenny Simms - Editing4Indies

❀ Created with Vellum

Authors

NOTE

We believe Delusional Dreams to be the right amount of suspense and spice. While we want you to enjoy, we also understand that your mental health matters most. Please be advised that we did our best to make sure all dark situations were noted and are included. This is a love story with a twist. It contains a cutting betrayal that can cause traumatic symptoms if not careful.

Content Warning! Delusional Dreams contains mature content that may not be suitable for all audiences. This book contains, but may not be limited to, the following triggers.

- Abuse of drugs with potential drug overdose and alcohol addiction
- Mental health
- Amnesia
- Forced therapy
- Questionable sexual consent with potential rape
- Somnophilia
- Explicit sexual situations

If you have any response to these triggers, please read with caution.

To that dream you really wish would
come true and finally turn into a reality.

PLAYLIST

- Am I Dreaming? – Metro Boomin
- Beautiful – Bazzi
- Breath – Telepopmusik
- Circles – Post Malone
- Counting Stars – OneRepublic
- Don't Wake Me I'm Not Dreaming – Young Joe
- Dreams – Fleetwood Mac
- Everest – Dream, Yung Gravy
- Fallin' for You – Colbie Caillat
- I Don't Know Why – NOTD, Astrid S
- Life is Beautiful – Thirty Seconds to Mars
- Mine – Bazzi
- Paradise – Bazzi
- Soul – Lee Brice
- Stay – iamjakehill
- Stuck – Thirty Seconds to Mars
- Sweet Dreams (Are Made of This) – Trinix
- Thing of Beauty – Danger Twins
- Was it a Dream? – Thirty Seconds to Mars
- Wildest Dreams – Taylor Swift

- You Make My Dreams Come True – Daryll Hall & John Oates

Delusional Dreams Spotify Playlist Link

Prologue

COLD, sharp leaves and sticks from the forest floor poke into my feet as I run. Briars pull at my hair, and thorns tug at my clothes. I push myself forward. The chill of the night seeps deep into my bones, removing the last traces of my warmth. My breath frosts in the air in front of me. Fog blankets the forest, and I can barely see my hand in front of my face. No light from the moon is filtering down through the thick forest canopy tonight. Nor can I see any stars twinkling above the leaves.

Faster. I need to run faster. I'm already pushing myself to the limit, but I must run. I have to get away. I force my legs to move, to propel my body forward.

My mind is a whirlwind of emotions and colors. All I know is I must keep moving, to go faster and farther before I am caught. I can't remember what is chasing me and why I'm running. I just know I cannot stop. I cannot let him catch me.

In the back of my mind, I wonder how I know, but I do know it's *him* who is chasing me. But…. "Who is he?" I ask myself as I try to increase my speed, my memory lapsing. How can I know but not know?

No matter how fast I go, I can hear him behind me. The

rhythmic beat of footsteps. The sound booms over and over again as he chases me. Like thunder chasing lightning. Occasionally, there is a step out of place, a syncopation that disrupts the harmony, the rush of almost being caught. The feeling that he almost has me trapped in his grasp, caught in his clutch.

He was several feet away at first, but now I can feel him at my heels. I can sense him reaching out to grab me and yank me deeper into the forest.

A soft whisper grazes my shoulder, caressing my neck before flowing into my ear. "Livi…"

The voice causes me to pause. *'Who?'* I voice to myself as I turn my head around.There he is, his imposing stature directly behind me. Giant onyx eyes, the color of the deepest ocean, peer right at me. Like Vanta black, no light escapes his blown-out pupils.

Shocked at the intensity of his gaze, I stumble over a root, free-falling into a tumble. I try to correct my balance by rotating my torso, but this only causes me to launch myself farther into the air. Slowly, I see the jagged edges of scattered rocks approaching as gravity brings my body to the forest floor. I already know that the fall will hurt long before my head hits the ground. Right before contact, I hear his voice, louder this time, as if he is screaming for me. "LIV!!!!!" And then all the world goes dark.

CHAPTER
One

THE SOUND of my alarm jolts me awake from the nightmare. I slam a clammy palm onto the clock to silence the alert. Dammit, the dreams have been getting worse lately. I look at my phone and see the time, rubbing my temples as the familiar throb set in. It's 5:00 a.m. *Ughh, why do I have to wake up so early?* I fucking hate waking up with a headache.

It's still dark outside, and I want to stay in bed for at least a few more hours. I'm not ready to get up and head to the shop. There are so many bouquet orders to complete today. But alas, 'tis the life of a florist—early hours and never-ending flower arrangements. It's why I named my shop *Morning Glory Arrangements*, after all. I've never been much of a night owl.

I sigh, then stretch, feeling my bones pop when an arm sneaks through my middle, and a man's hand wraps around my stomach. Then, I feel his lips on my neck.

I pause, slightly confused, and shake my head to try to clear the lethargy of my dreams and move past the fog of this morning's migraine. I don't remember… well, I don't think I know what is happening, but curiosity has me wondering who's in bed with me.

Luckily, I don't have to wait long to find out as the man snuggles deeper into my neck, whispering huskily, "Ana, good morning, my love," as he trails his fingers from my stomach to my breasts.

My breath hitches as his index finger and thumb pinch my left nipple, causing just enough pain to bring pleasure as I arch my back into him.

"Morning," I breathily reply just as he gives my right nipple the same attention as my left.

Kissing along my neck to my ear, my mystery man asks, "Did you sleep well?" as he continues his perusal of my breasts. My headache forgotten to the sensations he's bringing me.

"Yes," I moan as I force myself to turn toward the man so I can look at him. It feels so good to be lying here, letting him continue his pleasing pursuit, but I need to see him. As I gaze up and look into his eyes, the brightest blue skies reflect at me from the depths of his irises. While I'm mesmerized by the kaleidoscope of blues staring back at me, my memories slowly return, breaking through the blanket of sleep holding them hostage.

I smile. "And if you keep doing that, my dear husband, we'll never get out of this bed, and we both have to be at work early today. I need to get ten dozen bouquets, thirty table toppers, and a massive centerpiece ready for the Pearson's bridal shower this evening at The Club. And you, dear, have patients and families who need your counseling services or whatever it is therapists do at the office." I end the last with a bit of sass even though I know he is a well-known and highly sought after psychiatrist.

He groans. "I think staying in bed is just the perfect excuse for not working today and avoiding all those hassles." He pushes his hardening length against my thigh. "Don't you agree?"

I do, I really do, and I don't. I had to jump through hoops

to get the Pearson wedding contract, and it will take every ounce of energy and time to have the flowers in place before the seven thirty dinner. But I really want to stay here, wrapped up in this warm cocoon. Sighing once more, I tilt my head up and press a soft kiss on his lips. "Of course, I agree…"

"But…?" He continues for me.

"But we have to get up, honey. Come on, I'll make coffee and put our lunch together," I tell him with one last kiss before I roll to my side to get off the bed.

I don't make it far before he pulls me back, pushing me into the mattress, and fiercely claims my lips. Instinctively, I open for him, our tongues clashing as he pushes our kiss deeper. I run my hands through his thick golden waves, anchoring him to me as my legs wrap around his waist. But just as quick as our kiss begins, he lifts away, removes my legs from around him, and says, "Okay, fine, I'm going to go take a shower, a *very* cold shower, so you better promise me that we will continue this"—he pats my sex with his palm— "when we get home."

"I promise." My insides clench in anticipation of this evening's festivities.

"I love you, Ana Murphy."

"I love you, too, Bastian Murphy."

Sighing, I smile as I watch my husband walk to the bathroom naked. I can see his perfect, tight ass and ripped back. I'm really tempted to go after him and climb him like a tree, but dammit, it's time to get ready for work.

———

After I'm ready, I go to the kitchen to prepare breakfast for us. I pour us coffee and make sure Bastian has his lunch packed with leftover pasta. I'm gazing out the window and drinking my coffee when Bastian approaches me from behind and wraps his arms around my waist. He kisses me on the neck. "You smell so good, baby. I really want to stay here and just fuck you everywhere in this house. On the countertop, the kitchen table, fuck baby, I could just pound you into the floor."

With a smile, I glance at him over my shoulder, and tell him, "I wish we could. Believe me, if I didn't have that big order, I would say fuck it and roll around the carpet with you, but I can't bail on the Pearson's order, and you know it. I've worked too hard to secure their contract."

Bastian sighs. "I know, baby. I can't wait to get home tonight. I want you ready for me because I'm not going to be gentle with you, okay?" He presses his hips into my ass, grinding his hard-on against me.

A moan slips out of my mouth. Ohhh, I believe I can be okay with that. "Yes, sir." My mind plays out all of the naughty things he emphasizes with that simple motion.

"What a good girl you are, baby," Bastian says while squeezing my waist. Kissing underneath my ear, he strokes his hands up my sides, moving up to my breasts. Damn this man, he's making me so horny that I'm really considering staying home with him. If I just twist around, I could climb him like a tree while he holds me against the wall and…

When I'm about to suggest that he stays home, Bastian lets me go and stands back. I turn around to face him only to have his lips on mine, kissing me senseless before he releases me.

"Have a great day, baby, and I'll see you tonight," he states before he slaps my ass. Then he's out the door in a poof, gone.

CHAPTER
Two

THE SMELL of breakfast food wakes me up. Buttery goodness permeates the air. I can literally taste the warmth of biscuits.

I can hear the sizzle of bacon crisping and the pops of grease. My stomach rumbles as I roll toward the direction of the sounds.

As I'm turning, I notice my surroundings. It's dark wherever I am, but warm. Dim, twinkling firefly lights drape down from a vaulted ceiling. In the middle is a skylight where the first rays of the sun are streaming in, casting a glow downward. The walls are solid round logs, giving the room a cozy, rustic feeling. As I continue in my perusal, I see heavy, dark purple curtains belted closed over what must be windows.

The bed I'm currently lying in feels so soft yet firm, as if it was made specifically for me. A deep-sapphire comforter covers dark-emerald sheets that feel like velvet. I'm surrounded by a cloud of plush silk with plenty of pillows. It makes me wonder how deeply I can feel the individual textures of the threads as I rub the covers between my fingers; even the colors seem more vibrant as I look around.

My senses feel alive, as if they have been suppressed and are finally awake to the kaleidoscopic world around me. I arch my back into the mattress, slightly moaning at the sensory overload. I feel so much, my body tingles from the sensations of observation.

DING! A timer goes off, echoing from a corner that's not in my line of sight. I'm pulled out of my own rapture and reminded of the delicious smells that woke me up. As I finish rotating toward what I'm guessing must be the kitchen I realize that the entire area in this cabin is a large open layout.

Opposite the bed on the other side of the cabin hangs a solitary light above a blackened cast iron stove.

There. In the corner next to the stove, is a man. Eyes the color of the blackest night peer back at me from under long, shaggy bangs. His hair is a dark, wild mess. A shudder rumbles through my core. Fuck, whoever he is, he is so sexy.

My heart beats fast as we silently stare at each other. An unknown wanting beckons from deep within me, calling to him. Begging me to know more with a trembling need that I know only he can fulfill.

"Who… are you? Where am I?" I ask, slightly shaking.

"You're at home." He tilts his head a little. "What do you last remember?"

"Running. I was running and scared," I reply, sinking under the covers as I realize I don't know this man. "I remember being terrified and confused. So very confused. I think I'm still confused. Who are you again?"

"Sooo… you don't remember anything before you ran into the forest?" he asks. "And you don't remember me bringing you home?"

Home? I shake my head. I can't remember anything. Everything is fuzzy, incomplete.

The man puts down the kitchen tongs and walks over to the bed. As he gets closer, I notice how tall he is. He must be over six-two, maybe even six-four. His shoulders are so broad. I start to wonder what he would look like under the white shirt he has on. Well, not a shirt, more like a blouse, but who cares when you can see the muscular ridges of his collarbone peeking through. I lick my lips. I'm hungry, but I don't think it's for food. The man hovers over me now, his dark eyes glaring down at me. His full lips are tightened into a grimace like he doesn't know how to continue.

"Would you like to eat? I made your favorite breakfast of bacon, runny eggs, and biscuits."

"How… how do you know my favorite breakfast?" He was right, but how?

The confused look on my face must have told him something he needed to know because he simply sighed. "Livi, come over here to the table. We will talk as you eat."

"Livi?"

The man's frown deepens. He reaches out his hand to tuck a stray piece of hair behind my ear. The intimate move feels so familiar, I instinctively lean into his palm. He joins me on the bed, sitting on the edge while I'm still laying back. Grabbing my hands with his, he holds them tight as he looks me in the eyes. "You, my morning glory, are Livi. MY Livi," he says with emphasis, "and I'm YOUR Jace. Come on, join me at the table. I don't know what is going on in your beautiful head, but I know I at least have some answers that should help explain us. And maybe you already have some answers for your own questions."

Tentatively, I nod and climb out of bed. I immediately notice I'm only wearing a man's dark blue shirt that barely covers my ass. Angling my head down, I close my eyes and smell the shirt. Musky amber, woodsy, salty scents fill my nose, invading my nostrils, and heavily bombarding my senses with comfort and safety. The reminiscent memories of a distant place, a ocean perhaps… I can almost hear laughter floating on a breeze…

Grabbing onto my hands, Jace tugs and pulls me towards

the other side of the room. I join Jace at a small round table where he moves to put the final touches on the most delight-ful-looking buttered biscuits I have ever seen.

My stomach growls in response, thanking Jace in advance. Carefully, I pick up the piece of biscuit and take a bite. My mouth explodes with sunshine. I can taste the droplets of oil that grease the biscuit. How can my senses be this strong, this intense? It's fucking bread, and right now, it's the most deli-cious thing I've ever had in my mouth. I moan loudly.

Well, I think its the most delicious thing until I look across the table at Jace. Then I begin to salivate for a different reason. This guy, whoever he is, is absolutely gorgeous. Long lashes frame dark eyes that I know can see into the depths of my soul. Full, rosy lips surrounded by a dark scruff tells me Jace hasn't shaved in a few days. As I continue to stare, Jace smirks. My heart stops beating in my chest, and my mouth drops open, causing Jace to smile. And there goes my brain, short-circuited and no longer functioning. Heat floods my body and goes straight for the area between my thighs. I clench them together, hoping to hide this sudden wave of desire. I'm firmly, absolutely twitterpated.

Dammit, this man must have some sort of power over me because I can't stop checking him out, and he knows it. Just as I think I can muster some courage to avert my eyes from his face, Jace stands and reaches over to cup my chin. He pulls my face closer to his and leans down before pressing our lips together.

At first, I just sit there, dumbstruck. But then a warm feeling courses through my body, directly connecting my sex to my lips. Before I can stop myself, I stand and kiss Jace back ferociously.

However, Jace doesn't let our kiss go too far, just enough to satisfy some unknown need I could feel permeating through us both. Who is this guy, and why do I feel this way? And when did I straddle his lap?

"Livi," Jace says as he picks up a piece of bacon and presses it to my lips. "Eat. We apparently have a lot to discuss, and I think I better start with how we know each other."

"Okay," I reply as I take a bite. Immediately, the bacon's flavor makes me moan, but this doesn't faze Jace. He doesn't move me from his lap either. Instead, he keeps an arm banded around my waist as he brings another bite of the bacon to my lips. He grins when I moan again, then he picks up a forkful of eggs and feeds me that, too.

Jace continues to feed me until I'm about halfway done with my meal. I cannot deny how nice it is. Being held in his embrace while luxuriating in flavors so tantalizing, I can't hold back the sounds as I digest each bite. I grind downward in Jace's lap. "Oh, this is soooooo good."

Jace pauses, I can fill him hardening under me. The look on his face is one filled with many questions. Rather than asking, he just groans and simply states, "You, Oliviana, my seductively delicious woman, YOU are *my mate*. And the last thing I remember before you ran away, Livi... was me waiting at the end of the aisle on our wedding day. And this... Livi, this is our home in the mountains that we built together."

Before I can reply, his lips are on mine again, and the world explodes into stars.

CHAPTER
Three

THE ALARM BLARES; it cannot be time to wake up already. Groaning, I turn in bed. I'm so tired. Yesterday was rough. A flowered-filled day with lots of work at the shop, and I didn't think I was going to make it. My body hurts everywhere after the Pearson event. Not to mention all the places I was poked while trimming thorns.

That's when I remember, the motherfucker! That bastard.

I'm so mad. I mean madder than mad can be mad.

Sitting up quickly, I shove Bastian. "What the fuck? When did you get home, and why the hell didn't you call me or wake me up when you got here?"

"Huh…?" Bastian questions, still on the edge of sleep. "Babe, Ana, I told you I would be home late. You had to work late, too, so I thought we were on the same page."

"No. We were not. Yes, we had to work, and I had to work late, but you never said you would be late. When I got home, I tried to call and text you, but you didn't respond. So I went to bed. And now, here you are. I have no idea when you even got here. What the fuck, Bastian?"Bastian looks at me and says, "Babe, I got home around ten o'clock last night and saw you sleeping. I didn't have the heart to wake you up. I really wanted to, but I knew you had a hard day yesterday, and I was so busy with back-to-back appointments at the clinic and then my battery died. I'm so, so sorry, baby. I didn't mean to upset you."

I'm fuming because there is no excuse for what he did. Yesterday morning, he got me all hot and bothered. I spent the whole day thinking about it and plotting all of the sexy things that I wanted to do to him when we got home, but he never showed up. So excuse me if I'm mad. I have needs and get cranky when I don't get what I want, especially if I have the lady version of blue balls. You know those people who get hungry and angry because they have not eaten? Well, it's something like that but worse than being hangry.

I give Bastian a look that says he's in trouble, and he just smiles at me. Ughh, that fucking beautiful smile kills me every time, and he knows it.

Bastian pulls himself to my side of the bed and touches my face. "Baby, I really am sorry. I promise it won't happen again. Next time, I'll wake you up and ravage you all night long." Then he kisses me, and even though I'm still mad, I can't help myself,I kiss him back.

———

"Girl, let me tell you what Adrian did with his tongue last night! And then the way he twisted his fingers!" Janet tells me as we put away snips and clippers after finishing the last bouquets at *Morning Glory Arrangements*.

Janet is my number one employee. Okay, my only employee and probably, my best friend. Okay, like seriously, best friend in the world type of friend. And she shares way too much with me, like now.

"Seriously, Ana. The things that boy can do. I came twice before we even started to fuck. And he didn't even use fingers! I mean, that one time with the pinky was unbelievable, but now just his tongue!"

"Geez, Janet! I really don't need to know all that," I tell her.

"But you do, you really do." Janet continues. "Besides, I've seen Bastian. I can easily and happily imagine all the things that his body can do."

"Janet… seriously. I can't talk about your sex life right now, and I don't need to know your fantasies about my husband when I'm not even getting my own…" I trail off, hoping that Janet will have an ADHD moment and continue the conversation in a different direction, but nope, she knows me too well.

Giving me a hard look up and down, Janet asks, "Oh, fucking hell, Ana, what did Bastian do this time?"

This time? How often do I find myself complaining to Janet about Bastian?

"It's not that, Janet. It's just… I don't know. Yesterday, the man got me all ramped up for a lust-filled night and then didn't come home. He didn't even answer my texts. It was like he just disappeared. When I woke up this morning, he was in bed and all apologetic, but I just don't know. Something feels off."

"Are you pregnant?"

"Um, no, Janet. Definitely not pregnant."

"Okay, so what is it? Are you sleeping?"

"I'm not talking about me, Janet. I'm talking about Bastian. Something is off. And I don't know what."

"Whatever, Ana. You're just being silly; Bastian is crazy about you and worships the ground you walk on. I think you just need to get laid." Janet continues. "Besides, ever since…" Janet trails off.

"Ever since what?"

"You know. Since the accident."

"What accident? What the hell are you talking about, Janet? I don't remember an accident."

"I know, I know," Janet explains. "It's why we try not to mention it around you. You get really upset, and Bastian thinks it's best…"

"Why would Bastian think what's best and what accident? What am I missing?" I'm starting to get upset. What accident is she talking about, and why would Bastian tell her not to talk to me about it? Janet is my best friend; we talk about everything.

"Look, Ana. Stay calm and don't get mad. I know you cannot remember. But about six months ago, you were on your way home and had a terrible car wreck. We still don't know exactly how you drove off the road, but you got a nasty concussion. Since then, you've had strange mood swings, can be forgetful, and get very volatile when we try to discuss what happened prior to the accident."

I listen to what Janet is telling me but find it hard to believe. I'm searching my memory, and I don't remember. I'm getting angry. Maybe she's right because the more I think about what she's telling me, the angrier I feel. My fists clench at my sides, and I can feel my face heating.

"Look, Ana. I'm not trying to upset you. Take some deep breaths. Here, let me make you some hot tea. Do you want peach or rose hip?"

I watch Janet move over to the tea kettle that's on one of the benches in the back of the shop. I'm still trying to wrap my head around everything that she just said. When she looks back at me, I remember her question. "Peach please," I say quietly as I move to my favorite work chair and sit down.

"So… I had an accident."

"Yeah. And we tell you about it, but then you forget. Your memory has been affected the worst. It's like you know your workday and what you need to do, but sometimes you geek out and get freaky weird. Either way, don't worry about Bastian. The man is over the moon for you. You may not remember, but he never left your side the entire time you were in the hospital. I'm still surprised he's actually letting you walk to work alone since you refuse to drive now."

Janet is still going on, but I stop her with a question of my own.

"How long ago did he start letting me walk to work alone?"

"Oh. Well, hmm… yesterday."

I stare at Janet as this information sinks into my brain. "So up until yesterday, Bastian has been walking or driving me to work every day for the past few months?"

"Yeah! Quite romantic, too. I don't know why you stopped him from bringing you today. He always gets you coffee, and you always send him away with a flower…"

Janet continues giving her explanation, but I can no longer focus on what she was saying. How did I forget that Bastian brought me to work these past few weeks? Was I the one being the bitch this morning when he's been working his ass off to take care of me, and I can't even remember?

My head pounds. These migraines must be an after-effect of the accident. I shake my head, trying to remove the discomforting layer pressing in from all sides as my vision darkens.

CHAPTER
Four

THE ANNOYING CHIRPING of birds rouses me awake. The sounds are so intense that I can pick out individual notes and tones. I can hear their various sonnets coaxing me from the world of dreams as they weave their melodic harmonies. A soft light from the window illuminates the smoldering fireplace where I can still hear the last crackling embers die down for the day. Stretching out my fingers, I find a familiar feeling of luxurious bedding. Sighing, I stretch my body and sink deeper into the covers. I love this bed. This bed loves me. I know because this bed gives me the best mattress hugs—and oh, the smell. I inhale deeply, catching remnants of amber musk floating in the woods along the coast with hints of saltiness from a drifting sea breeze. This aroma belongs to only one male, my mate.

I sit up quickly with a smile on my face and look around the room for Jace. However, I don't see my mate anywhere. Getting out of bed, I straighten out the shirt I was wearing. I don't remember putting the shirt on, so Jace must have changed me after dinner last night.

Damn, that kiss! It was so incredible that it's the only

thing my mind can focus on as I wander across the open floor to a door that I think is the bathroom.

Luckily, it is. Rustically romantic, the bathroom has been modernized to be inviting and place to truly relax.. The first thing I notice as I step inside is the large walk-in shower that leads into a sunken pool that must be big enough to fit six people. Jets and shower heads are abundant with a floor-to-ceiling window that looks out into the fog-laden forest. It makes me wonder if Jace would be willing to try out the pool and freshen up with me later after I find him.

Putting my sexy thinking to the side, I make my way to the second thing I spot, a toilet.

After doing my business, I rummage around in some drawers next to a freestanding sink, looking for a toothbrush and comb. The first drawer contains strange bottles of glittering elixirs. I don't recognize any of them, but when I open one that glows bright blue, it smells like blueberries and coffee. That's weirdly odd.

Putting that one down, I open a red bottle that looks as if it contains blood. It's thick and gooey, and smells like toasted marshmallows and strawberries.

Hmm. Interesting.

Moving on from the first drawer, I open the second drawer only to find a variety of toys. Shocked and intrigued, I pick up the first phallic-shaped object with a dangling sucker attached. *What is this guy into?* I wonder as I look down at the assortment of balls strung together and other strange, feathered items.

Closing the second drawer of naughty oddities, I open the next drawer and finally find a spare toothbrush and toothpaste. Thank the sprites, I do not do dragon breath.

Standing up to brush my teeth, I move over to the sink. When I look up into the mirror, I realized that the green in my eyes looks dull. I haven't been sleeping well. Vivid, nightmares are making my sleep restless even though Jace has been loving and taking care to exhaust my body every night.

As I contemplate my appearance, something sparkling around my neck catches my eyes. Shoving my strawberry-blond hair to the side, I pick up a delicate, iridescent chain resting along my collarbone. On the chain is a single, simple pendant that contains a black pearl encased in a copper nest with the deepest green emerald, cut perfectly to its namesake, sitting on top. Something familiar transfixes me as I gaze at the necklace…

"Did Jace give me this?" I ask out loud to no one. Mesmerized, I tug the necklace off around my head to get a better look. Peering deep into the emerald, I see bright red and yellow flames dancing within the facets. I'm so focused that I don't realize the pendant starts to heat. Before I can ask why, the jewels becomes so hot that I drop the entire necklace onto the floor mat at my feet.

Immediately, a fire sparks from the pendant and begins raging on the rug. Trying to think fast, I look around the bathroom for a fire extinguisher but cannot find one. Running into the central part of the cabin, I cannot find one there either, so I grab a glass of a clear liquid I see sitting on the counter and run back to the bathroom. The fire has already grown and threatens to move toward the main living space. I toss what I'm assuming is water onto the flames only to be met with an explosive backlash. I apparently just fueled the fire's vigor.

Screaming like a crazy banshee, I'm desperate to find something to stop the fire.

I start coughing and can't stop. Every breath is a struggle as smoke fills the cabin. I just know that I'm going to die in this bathroom if I don't stop the fire.

Suddenly, Jace grabs my arms from behind and moves me outside the bathroom. Sweeping me off my feet into a bridal hold, he turns around with me still in his arms before he raises his left hand. Water appears out of nowhere and moves around the room, quickly extinguishing the fire in less than a minute.

I'm absolutely dumbfounded. What the fuck just happened? Where did all the water come from? Am I going crazy?

I look around the room and see everything drenched in water. There is no more fire, just the remnants of smoldering steam rising up.

Jace finally puts me on the floor and turns me to face him. Pulling me to his chest, he cradles my face, asking, "Livi, are you okay?"

His eyes roam up and down my body, looking for injuries, but I have none. When his perusal brings his eyes back to my face, I tell him, "Yes, I'm okay. How… how did you do that? Where did all that water come from? Am I seeing things? I'm so confused, Jace." I can feel a sob lodging in my throat as I'm getting more and more worked up because I don't under-stand what just happened.

"I did that. I put the fire out with my water powers," he explains.

I stare at Jace, giving him an inquisitive "I don't believe you" look even though I just witnessed him using water powers. As my gaze wanders up his body, I finally realize he has no shirt on. My heart stumbles, and I almost swoon. Oh, my goodness. He's a fucking masterpiece. Creamy, golden skin with abs for days, that downward V that leads toward a happy trail peeking from his pants. His chiseled chest is covered in one long, branching, arching tattoo that wraps around his left arm over to his back. An intricate wave that depicts a storm on the sea with a compass over his left pec navigating a tattoo of a ship to safety near a lighthouse.

"What powers?" I softly question as I reach out to stroke one of the waves of his tattoo. "What are you talking about?" I know my confusion must be written all over my face because Jace takes a moment to remind me of what I keep forgetting.

Jace moves us to a chair and pulls me into his lap. "Livi, you are my mate, and I'm yours. We are both Fae." Jace takes my hands in his, looking me deep into my eyes, and continues. "I'm a Water Fae, and you are an Earth Fae. We have powers based on our Fae traits. Because I'm Water Fae, I can control all water, while you can control all Earth elements."

I'm stunned, and in a panic, I start to ask, "Fae? Wait! What do you mean we're Fae? Are we in a fairyland or something like that? What do you mean I control Earth elements? Jace, this is just too unreal. It's like a dream."

I start touching my body all over, checking my form, but it feels human. I have legs, arms, breasts, a head, hair… I look up at Jace, and for the first time, I pay attention to more than his eyes. His ears are pointed, not curved. I reach up to trace the tip with my finger, then quickly touch my own. Also pointed. My breathing comes in harsh, ragged breaths. The world starts to spin, and a familiar ache threatens to appear at the back of my head.

"Shh, Livi. It's okay. Please, please don't panic. I'll explain everything. Focus, my love… Shhh, breathe with me."

"Liv, we are in the Fae Realm south of the the the City of Chrysoberyl. In this world, we have four types of Elemental Fae: Water, Earth, Fire, and Air. There are a few hybrids here and there mixed in with the various shifters and other Fae. You and I, well, we are from the royal Elemental Fae families.

There area multiple royal families, all governing a local section of their particular element or an area with a large amount of a certain population.

You, my mountain flower, are part of the Appalachian Earth Fae court where your parents, Oryan and Lydia Chamberlaine, rule over the Emerald Mountains. One day, your older brother Lucas will take over Chrysoberyl while you and I will rule my home, Quartzside, on the southern coast. My parents, Jackson and Celine Seaborne, rule over the coastal marshlands and the Gulf of Sapphire. My younger siblings will all eventually leave or stay, depending on what they want to do and if they find mates who need them to move.

A few years ago when we started to make our wedding and mating moon plans we needed to decide where we would live before becoming the new ruling monarchs. We knew we wanted to stay closer to your parents since ultimately you would make the move with me to the seashore.

We built our cabin in the mountains of Diopside, a four day journey on horse from the coast but only two to three days from your parents in Chrysoberyl. Perfectly situated on the top of Mount Lazuli, here we can be secluded while we start our family but close enough in order to attend court and spend time with friends and family.

When I returned to the cabin and saw the fire, I called my waterpower. I didn't mean to flood the place. I was so worried about you that I lost control of my water. Since our wedding day, you haven't been you, and I've been worried your heat is messing with your head."

Jace cradles my cheek at this point, and even though I'm trying to pay attention to what he's saying, I'm completely transfixed by his dark eyes until he mentions something about me being hot.

"Hot? No, Jace, I'm not hot. Just confused."

Jace rubs my back in an up-and-down motion. It feels like an attempt to calm us both down. But the movement causes tingles everywhere he touches.

"Oh, Livi, sweetheart. We're going to figure out what's going on, but I'm not saying that you're hot or there is too much heat. No love, your heat, as in you are going into heat. We planned our wedding ceremony around your first formal heat and built the cabin in a secluded area near your element so we could have our privacy. Do you understand?" Jace looks at me pleadingly, but I'm still confused.

"No, not really. What do you mean by my first heat?" I rotate in his lap, looking around at the cabin. I spot the bed and remember the scents and how comfortable it was. My libido skyrockets. I'm not sure what is happening to my body, but I can feel a hot fever spreading from my toes to my nose.

Jace turns me so I'm sitting, and he's between my legs. He grabs my face with both hands and tells me, "Livi, a female Fae's heat starts right after they turn twenty-four. It's when Fae can get pregnant, lasting each year from the first spring new moon to new moon for Earth Fae. I know you don't remember, and things are confusing, but I promise this is not a nightmare. It's a part of our plans for our dream to come true. Our happily ever after, Oliviana. Let me take care of you, my love, and everything will be okay."

Jace's words go straight to my core. Something about the way he tells me he will take care of me causes my sex to pound and clench. The heat coursing through my body burns brighter than the previous inferno in the bathroom. Jace moves into me, leaning forward, sniffing. "I can smell your arousal, mate."

An unfathomable desire rushes into me, driving me to the brink of rapture. I can't stop myself as I push my chest into Jace's. He mentioned something about being hot, and I'm burning on the inside for him. I'm barely millimeters from his lips pressing to mine when Jace drops to his knees. After he hikes my leg over his shoulder, his mouth finds my lower lips before he pulls me to his mouth and begins to kiss.

CHAPTER
Five

AROUSED AND SLICK, I think, *What a dream!* I stretch out my lower back, and it pops in such a good way, making me moan. My hand brushes up against a warm, solid chest.

Yum, I sigh in my mind as I rub my breasts and grind my ass against the hard body of the man behind me.

"Ana," a breathy whisper moans into my ear before he kisses the side of my neck, right in that sweet spot that makes me shiver.

Hands circle my breasts, fingers teasing my nipples as his hard length grows behind me. As I wiggle my ass against his cock, he slowly traces a pathway with his hand down from my breast. Slipping under my shorts, he dips between my thighs and parts my folds before rubbing my clit in sensuous circles. I moan as I arch more of my back into his front.

"So wet, so responsive," he tells me as he pushes a finger inside.

My pussy clenches around his finger as he moves it in and out, his thumb circling my clit as he nibbles on the back of my neck. He pushes two fingers inside, stretching, prepping.

"More," I demand. I need more. Turning me around so I'm on my back, he moves on top of me. Desire pools in the depths of his bright-blue eyes. His lips find mine in a hurried, frenzied kiss.

Pulling back, he asks, "Ana, I'm going to fuck you now. Are you ready?"

"Yes, please. I need you. Fuck me, please."

In one smooth motion, he thrusts inside. No matter how many times he's penetrated me, the first push always burns. He fills me completely, stretching me to a limit only he can. His forehead is next to mine, and his breaths mix with mine as he begins to slowly move.

Picking up speed, he takes one of my legs and puts it on his shoulders. "Fuck, Ana, you are so tight and deep. I love the way my cock feels and looks inside your pussy."

"Harder," I cry out. Leaning down, he latches his lips around my nipple and sucks before moving to the other breast. He's making me crazy with desire. Grabbing onto his back, I claw my fingers into his muscles. My pussy clenches so hard I can feel the beginning of an orgasm forming. I grip his ass, pulling him so he plunges deeper and harder into me, begging him for more. "Please, oh please, just let me come. Please make me come," I chant as he relentlessly pounds harder and faster. He's giving me everything I ask for, his hips hitting my clit as he thrusts forward.

His hand moves downward, and he pinches my hard little nub before he starts rubbing it, making quick circles. It's all I need to push me over the edge and detonate my climax.

"Bastian!" I scream out as my pussy milks his cock, drinking his release as his own orgasm powers through him and into me. I can feel his seed filling my womb.

He collapses on top of me, kissing and nuzzling my face and neck. "Oh, Ana. That was incredible."

Feelings of elation fill me as I kiss my husband back. "Eh, it was okay," I tease.

Bastian grins wickedly before saying, "Is that so?" before he begins to tickle me up and down my sides.

Giggling while trying to get him off me, I cry, "Stop! It was awesome, okay! It was a great orgasm. The dick of Bastian Murphy is perfect!"

"That's better," Bastian says as he stops tickling me and pulls me into an embrace. Kissing my lips, he tells me he loves me, then pulls me from the bed so we can get our day started. Slapping my ass as we walk to the bathroom, Bastian grabs me and tugs me into a backward hug before pressing a kiss to the side of my head and saying, "You have no idea how happy I'm that you are my wife, Ana. I promise to make all your dreams come true."

Bastian pulls me into the shower where we get dirty once more before we finally clean up and go to work.

———

Later that day at work, Janet and I are rearranging the shop after a large flower delivery when I got a delivery of my own. Grinning, I open the card that is attached to a rectangular box and read the message inside.

"For creating more sexy memories that are better than OKAY. - Love, B"

Curious, I laugh and lift the top off the box. Tissue paper falls out everywhere, revealing the tiniest, skimpiest piece of white lingerie I've ever seen. A one-piece bodysuit that looks like it will barely cover my ass and leaves no room to the imagination for my boobs.

"What have you got over there, my friend?" Janet asks as she saunters over to stand beside me. She grabs the lingerie from me and smiles as she wiggles her eyebrows. "Ohhh, look at this… I'm guessing everything is okay with Bastian?"

I look at her and don't know what to say. What does she

mean if things are okay with Bastian? Have they been wrong before? I think my face says what I'm thinking because she says, "Remember when we talked yesterday, you told me that you felt something was wrong with Bastian? I told you that you were crazy, and I was right. That man has good taste. This will look smoking hot on you. If I liked girls, I'd make you put it on here and prance around the displays."

Laughing at Janet's silliness, I remember I was upset yesterday because Bastian came home late the night before and never woke me up. He's just gone so much that it's frustrating.

"Yeah, I guess I was being dramatic."

Janet smiles and puts the lingerie back in the box before covering it with tissue paper. "Well, great to know because I guess that you're going to get fucked good tonight. Do you have any plans of what you want to do once you put this little thing on?"

Smiling back and thinking about my orgasmic morning, I tell Janet, "So... I'm thinking about getting home early to make dinner. Then wait for him to get home with only the lingerie on. What do you think? Or maybe I should still be cooking when he arrives. Or should I have an apron on over this? Heels or barefoot?"

I look at Janet, and she's nodding. "Yeah. I definitely think that should work. Having you still cooking when he gets home will be soooo sexy. Maybe apron, play with the look and see. Do you still have those knock-off white pleather Louboutin's? Because they would look so hot, all in white with just a hint of red."

"I do," I reply, mentally hoping he arrives home when he's supposed to. I know I'll be very mad if he doesn't come home on time. Maybe I'm hormonal, or perhaps it was the accident, or maybe it was the sex this morning that made me forget what he did yesterday, and now he's trying to make amends.

But this morning was extremely good, and I want a repeat of that.

We need these good moments in this life. We often fall prey to the deception that we can balance work and life. This denial leads to disruptions in our relationships. Bastian and I have had a rocky ride recently, and our marriage is a two-way highway, and maybe I've been the parked car. Unsure of which way to turn, I'm stalled out in my emotions, sitting at a fork in the road with my hazard lights blinking.

Changing my own mental tune, I allow myself to slip back into thinking happy sexy thoughts as I gear myself up for the evening.

Janet and I finish cleaning up the shop quickly so we can both leave early. I'm humming to myself as I flip the lights and lock the door. I'm beyond excited to start dinner and be ready in my new lingerie by the time Bastian comes home.

CHAPTER
Six

THOSE LIPS, that kiss.

Memories drift in and out, ebbing and flowing as each taste, lick, and flick rocks me back and forth toward ecstasy. Wave after wave of euphoria gently crashes into me, caressing my every facet, kissing every curve. I wonder if I'm but a lonely current, moving with the flow of this world.

Eyes, if that's what they are, observe a vast blue wilderness where bubbles swirl and stars swim. Giggles, laughter, and moans tease my auditory nerves. The sounds are tempting me to reach out and touch, to feel. A warmth like I've never experienced blankets me as I continue my blissful coast. Sighing, I breathe in a scent only I know so well. My woodland ocean—where even in the deep forest, you can smell the salty breeze floating in the wind.

As a river, I flood into a new reality. The force of my tide pours through the land, orgasming as life and awareness bring me back to the current, the present.

That kiss. This kiss.

Oh, THIS KISS!

A whimpering moan escapes my lips as I lose contact with the kiss. Pushing my hips up, I try to seek the connection and feel those lips once again at my core. I shudder as the residual climax wrings its way through my muscles. Giving up, I relax my body back onto the bed and open my eyes. Opulent onyx irises meet mine.

Grinning like a satisfied Cheshire cat, Jace leans over to rub his nose against mine. The wetness of my arousal coats my face as he rubs his scruff across my cheeks. I sigh in sweet content, luxuriating in the aroma of our combined essences. Mine a tangy honeysuckle, strawberry flavor swirled with the amber, saltiness of his musk.

"Good morning, my lovely glory. Sleep well?"

Nodding and sighing at his endearment, I respond, "Yes, my night owl. But I enjoyed waking up even more." I peck him on the lips, somewhat enjoying the combination of his muskiness with my own scent.

"I'm sure you did," he says with a wink. "Now come on. You've been sleeping enough lately. Let's go on an adventure and explore outside the cabin today." Jace pulls me to my feet before I can protest.

After he drags his shirt over my head, I ask him, "What did you do that for?"

"Why, my gorgeous mate? Because if I keep staring at those perfect tits any longer, I will drag you back to bed. And while I love fucking you endlessly for days at a time, this is the first morning in five days that you have been lucid and not wrapped around my cock. So that, my Livi love, is why I'm capitalizing on our mating moon"—Jace adds in quotations—"and taking you on an epic romantic adventure. Cock ready and primed, if necessary, when the mood strikes."

Then he slaps my ass and pushes me toward the bathroom to go get ready for a day filled with hiking, adventuring, and mating when the need arises.

My heart skips. He's the best damn dream ever.

———

Water splashes on my face. Laughing while trying to avoid gulping lake water should be labeled with caution. Ripples tickle my sides as a swell rises, nudging between my legs. Grabbing onto the stream of water between my thighs, I hold on tight. Jace casts his magic, creating an amusement park out of the crystal blue lake we found hiking up the face of a mountain near our cabin. Water pulls and pushes me around, creating dense enough matter I can hang on as it carries me on a thrill while also proving a protective cocoon.

We had been climbing over some boulders during the heat of the day when Jace saw the reflection of sunlight through the trees coming from some water. At the top of the crest, we were able to look down and see the most beautiful turquoise blue lake. Of course, we had to investigate and quench our thirst.

The water of the lake is so crystal clear I can see the various fish darting in between shadows of fallen trees and aquatic plants. Shiners flash like silver dollars while sunfish blaze in the light with their bright red strips. Dragonflies and Dobsonflies with purple and blue wings dance along the shore, weaving in and out of the grasses and they lightly touch down to kiss the water's surface. Butterflies in many sizes and spectrum of colors play among brightly yellow water irises. Other water bugs skid across the smooth surface, creating tiny ripples. Fluffy clouds are reflected back on the polished mirrored surface, creating the illusion that we could possibly be standing upside down. It's absolutely breathtaking

Dipping and racing, Jace uses his water magic to tease, taunt, and drive me around the lake as he elicits giggle after tormenting giggle from his "water tickling."

I'm racing to the farthest beach on a wave when I finally catch my breath and gain enough of my senses to snap back with my own defensive maneuver. I need to think fast. As an

Earth Fae, I should be able to do something to escape this watery roller coaster.

Breathing deep, I start calling deep inside my core, and I pull Earth energy into my essence. This feels amazing. It's like I can sense everything around me—the ground, the trees, the actual Earth, all my surroundings. Shaping the mud below the water, I hold out my hands in front of myself. Rotating my open palms, I imagine I'm forming balls of mud dough well below the surface, invisible and hiding out of sight.

Holding Jace's surging water wave with my legs as it brings me closer and closer to the shore, I use all my concentration to build, create, and accumulate. The wave breaches the shoreline and begins to reach its crest, the friction abruptly stopping the water's trajectory, bringing the apex of the wave tumbling back toward the ground. I release and strike.

Hundreds of small, medium, and large mud balls eject themselves out of the water. Hurtling upward, gravity brings them back down. Every single one of the balls of mud home in and target Jace. As I begin to flip with the rolling water, I have the epic pleasure of seeing my mate getting whacked with many of those pellets before he dives underwater to safety.

And here I was worried for a moment that I could not use my earth magic. That was easy, just like breathing. This power is not new; it is ingrained in me.

Laughing to myself, I watch Jace as he surfaces, smirking and thinking he outmaneuvered my play. Ha! Joke's on him. An underwater eruption causes Jace to turn around, trying to find the source of the sound. Too bad it is directly underneath my mate. An exponentially expanding mud tree sprouts and skyrockets Jace into the air before gravity deposits him directly into the middle of the lake. He pulls himself into a cannonball right before impact, causing a splash that reaches my feet.

Standing confidently at the edge of the shoreline, I watch my mate emerge from the water. Covered in mud, he stalks stealthily toward me. The predator in his eyes has only one prey in its sights. Me.

Laughing and screaming, I turn to run. I take three steps, but he's too fast. Jace snatches me out of the air before throwing me over his shoulder and uses his water magic to create a geyser that propels us high into the sky. Then we drop, falling back toward the lake. Holding me tight with a smile, Jace pulls me closer as we plunge. I tilt my face toward his and place my hand against his cheek. Our lips crash and tongues tangle as we splash down.

———

After we finally pulled ourselves out of the lake, Jace decided it was time to picnic.

As he unpacked our lunch, I looked around and saw how beautiful and peaceful it is here.

Moss-covered turtles peek their noses out from the still water surface, bubbles trailing behind them as they glide through the water. Thousands of rainbow-colored minnows and other shiner fish dart along the shore, causing a psychedelic prism as they jump from shadow to shadow, hiding from the birds above. There must be at least ten species of avians just in the trees above my head. Birds with large yellow beaks, others with sapphire blue and ruby red plumage, and even more with multifaceted tail feathers that reach down below the tree limbs where they are perched. I'm looking up into the trees and gazing at the star-shaped leaves when a fluorescent-green butterfly lands on my nose.

I sneeze before I giggle. It's a secret fact I'm obsessed with butterflies. It's also well-known that when a butterfly lands on you, it's a sign of good luck and great things to come. I remember my mother always telling me the Fae tale that butterflies carry the core of all Earth magic and that the butterflies only visit the most genuine and altruistic of Fae. They represent a blessing, gifted from where all power is created.

"Liv honey, lunch is ready. Come over here." Jace interrupts my daydreaming, and the butterfly flutters away into the sky.

My belly clenches with a different need as I get up to go over to where he has an entire buffet laid out for us. Just looking at Jace makes me want to have another type of lunch.

Yet Jace makes it abundantly clear that I need my sustenance for what he plans later when he looks at me and states, "My lovely morning glory, you have to stop looking at me that way. I'm not giving in because you need to eat food. I can see the desire in your eyes and smell your arousal from here, and I'm saying no. We have important plans later."

Reluctantly, I agreed, mainly because I really was hungry, and if the rest of the day is as fun as today, well, having sex could wait a little while. But only a little while. Like Jace said and had explained to me, we were on our equivalent of a honeymoon. We had been planning for years, waiting to officially bond on the new moon after my twenty-fourth birthday so we could turn the entire affair into our own personal "mating moon."

While Jace and I had definitely had adult affairs prior to our bonding, this was special because we were both ready to take on our royal responsibilities. And secretly, we were more than ready to start a family. Even before we knew each other intimately, we would play with names for girls, boys, sets of multiples, planning for the one or many children we would one day raise. It was a natural course in our relationship.

Now that I'm thinking about baby names, I start to remember why Jace calls me Livi. When I was a toddler, I couldn't say my full name because it was way too complicated for my young voice. Around two, I met Jace for the first time. When he asked me for my name, I tried so hard to say Oliviana, but all I could get out was "Wivii."

"Cute," he replied. "I'm Jace Seaborne." I remember the wind whipping by us, holding us together in a combined twister of air and water as I gazed back at him, feeling the way Jace crossed my tongue before breaking the magic and fumbling out 'Ja-seeeea.'

From that day forward, Jace called me Livi. I liked it so much that I became Livi to all my close friends and family.

I phase out of my daydream and notice the enticing buffet in front of me.

Jace has laid out various fruits, cheeses, and breads on a blanket that he has positioned under a tree near the lake. The vision is full of nostalgia, reminding me of another one of our first meetings. The day our mothers went on a picnic together at the lake. Jace and his family were visiting us in the forest. They had traveled from the ocean, and I could still smell the saltiness of the sea coating his skin. I might have been five years old at the time. But as soon as I saw the dark-eyed, petulant little boy hanging onto his mother's skirts, I knew in that moment he was forever mine and that I would be the thief and keeper of his heart. That day, the ground shook and a tidal wave crashed to shore where we stood. Our mothers simply exchanged knowing nods with each other, grins stretching ear to ear.

"Mates," one of our mothers stated. "Why, yes indeed, mates they are," agreed the other. Whose mother said what never mattered because, from that day on, our lives were planned together, constantly intertwined when able and connecting us with more than just values, but with interests and talents to complement our juvenile powers.

"I cannot believe you did that," I complain to Jace as I try to twist as much water out of my hair as possible before I take my seat on the blanket. Luckily, we were smart and had removed all our clothes before playing in the water. Who knew skinny-dipping could be so adventurous?

"You know," I tell Jace, "all that water power. You could just pull it out of my air and dry me out."

"I could. But I really do love seeing you all wet." Jace winks at me.

Dammit, he's good. I roll my eyes to hide my slowly melting heart.

CHAPTER
Seven

DREAMS. Such fickle things. My heart races as I wake up to my alarm. Watery scenes and laughter fading from my memory as I surface toward consciousness.

It's 5:00 a.m. already, again...

I can't remember the full details of the dream as I turn off the annoying buzz. But I do know I'm frustrated. Rolling over, I find the other side of my bed cold and empty.

I feel resigned but impatient. Bastian has been growing more and more absent. I can't remember the last time we were both at home in the evenings and went to bed together.

Making my way to the bathroom, I do my morning routine and head downstairs.

I'm surprised when the smell of coffee hits my nostrils. I inhale deeply, enjoying the delicious nutty aroma. As I continue my trek, I can see the glow of lights from the kitchen and hear sizzles and pops coming from something on the stove. Smoky, buttery goodness greets me as I enter the space to find Bastian cooking.

Dressed only in dark gray sweatpants that hang low on his hips, Bastian concentrates too hard on the bacon popping in the skillet to notice me approaching from behind.

All irritation leaves me as I wrap my arms around his waist, pressing my front against his back.

"Good morning, husband. What did I do to earn this treat?"

Bastian rotates and turns to face me, cupping my cheek in his hand and leaning down to quickly kiss my lips.

"Morning, wifey. Did you sleep well?"

"It was okay," I replied. "I didn't like waking up alone and cold. But seriously, Bastian, you never cook breakfast. What's up?"

"What, I can't treat my wife just for being my wife? I thought you deserved something special. I know the past several months have been rough, and I think we've been losing ourselves lately. We're both finally off together today, so I'm taking you on an all-day date. And then I'll fix the problem of that cold bed you don't like."

I look at my husband quizzically. I'm excited, but at the same time, this is not his normal. I decide that I will go with the flow because I think he's right. I think we have been so focused on work and routine that we need a change, we need to reconnect.

"Bastian, I'm so sorry. I know recently I have been a bitch to you. I know you are working very hard, and sometimes I'm very demanding."

"Sweetheart, what are you talking about?"

"Bast, I know I've been a raging bitch, and I'm just trying to apologize." I continue my rant. "Like a few days ago when I woke up angry and then woke you up to argue about you not waking me up to have sex. Sometimes I just feel... weird. It's like I lose myself and don't think rationally."

He stands in front of me and kisses me softly on the lips.

"I understand, my love. Ever since the accident... it's been this way. But it's getting better. Your mind is healing, so I have a fun day planned for us. Once we finish eating, you are going to get ready because we're going to the lake today."

The lake… a glimpse of the dream I had last night buzzes in my mind.

Bastian turns me around and slaps my ass, pushing me toward the table. "Sit. I will bring you breakfast in a minute."

I walk to the table and sit down like the good wife that I am.

"What are we going to do at the lake today?" I ask Bastian while he serves up the breakfast and comes to the table with two plates.

He scrambled some eggs with veggies, bacon, and toast. It smells delightful, and I greedily dig into the delicious meal. I moan around a bite of bacon and glance up to see Bastian swallowing as he glares at me.

Clearing his throat, I send him a knowing grin and waggle my eyebrows as he explains our plans.

"I thought we could rent a paddleboard and fish a little bit. I already packed us lunch so we can have a nice picnic. I plan to have fun with you today and later when we get home…" Bastian pauses with an eyebrow wiggle of his own. "I'll make up for my absences and have some sexy time with you. Maybe even finally see you show off the new lingerie I got you. You know white is my favorite color."

"That sounds nice." I can't contain my grin. "I really love to paddleboard, but the fishing not so much. That's all you, boo. But I'll watch you attempt to reel in something while I explore."

I don't like fishing. I find it extremely boring, and I definitely don't like touching the wiggly, gross worms. Just because I'm a florist doesn't mean I like all things that you can find in the dirt. I shiver just imagining having to hook one of those earth diggers. But, I sigh, I know Bastian loves to fish, so I guess I'll have to suck it up because I really do like to float around on a paddleboard. Hmm… maybe I can catalog some of the local flora and fauna as I drift.

Bastian looks down at me and smiles. Sometimes I forget how his six-one frame towers over my tiny five-five.

"I know you don't like to fish, Ana, but you go and enjoy the sun while I do the fishing. I definitely have plans on hooking… some things"—he naughtily grins—"and enjoy looking at your delectable body in that hot little bathing suit you purchased last summer. That way we are still doing something that we both enjoy together."

Oh, so he just wants to ogle me while he fishes. But what can I say, I kinda like that idea, too. Especially when I start to think of Bastian in nothing but his swim trunks and those flat, washboard abs on display. Maybe I'll do some ogling of my own.

"Okay, let's do that. Hurry up and finish breakfast. I'm so excited!"

Leaning forward, I press a peck on Bastian's lips. I'm deviously planning my entire outfit because I know he won't be able to concentrate with me beside him (ha! Men, so predictable), but I will let him think what he wants, and I'll give him some bait if fishing is what he wants.

After we finish eating breakfast, I put the plates in the dishwasher and head to our room to change. I dig around my dresser drawers and find the sexiest piece of clothing I own. A simple white one-piece swimsuit. It has a low V-cut on the front showing off my perky breasts and super low swoop in the back. Just enough that my ass cheeks poke out and make it look like a thong. It drives Bastian wild, so I'll take the discomfort of walking around with nylon up the crack of my ass.

After I put on my swimsuit, I look at myself in the mirror and decide to add some shorts, sandals, big sunglasses, and an even bigger white hat. Then I let my hair loose, spritz a little water, and rake my fingers through until I have nice long waves. I'm done and ready to go.

There is a bounce to my step as we leave for our day-date adventure.

————

Today is a wonderful day to spend at the lake. I mean, the weather is absolutely spectacular. Just like a perfect day in April. The sky is clear, it's not too hot, it's not too cold, and the sun feels great on my body. This lake is beautiful. Nestled in a valley with mountains in the background, there is a huge area to sit and picnic under the pine and oak trees.

A few families have already found spots. Coolers and baskets adorn tables while parents watch their children playing at the shoreline. It's so pleasant.

Bastian has a strong grip on my hand and tugs me toward the boathouse. "Come on, Ana. Why are you so distracted?"

"Bast, what's the rush? It's so nice out here. I just wanted to look around and enjoy the moment."

But he continues to pull me forward with him.

At the boathouse, we rent a paddleboard for me and a kayak for him. While Bastian pursues the various tackle he wants to add to his collection, I thank the young guy for helping us. I turn to walk to the lake, but an angry Bastian immediately confronts me.

"What's wrong?" I ask.

His glare is full of fury. "You could have been less flirty with that guy. I was standing right there beside you. Don't you have any consideration for my feelings?"

I'm absolutely shocked because I don't know where this is coming from. "What? I was not flirting with anyone." What the hell is Bastian talking about? A part of me wants to slap him. The other part is just confused by this behavior. The guy was just helping make sure we had all of our gear, and I was being nice.

"Well, that's not what it looked like to me. You were all smiles and touching your hair while he talked to us."

"Touching my hair?" I start.

"Yes, Ana…" Bastian snarks back. "You were touching your hair and pushing your boobs up into his face. Or you lean over so he can see *all that belongs to me*."

"For real, Bastian? Whatever, I really was not. Besides, why would I do that? I'm right here with you and wouldn't do that to you. I was just being nice and polite. I was not trying to come off as flirty." Rolling my eyes, I add quotations around my last words.

"You could have fooled me, Ana. I planned this whole day for us, and this is how you act. What's wrong with you?"

"What the fuck is wrong with me, Bastian Murphy? What the fuck is wrong with you?" I'm screaming at him now. My anger is ready to explode and implode us all. Damn him and his fucking jealousy. He's acting like I'm a fucking whore who would cheat on him with any man. I haven't even looked at anyone since we've been together. I can't even remember any guy before Bastian, that's how much he eclipses my heart. I stomp off, tears threatening to pour out of my eyes.

I stop in front of the beach and put my paddleboard on the sand. Turning around, I look at Bastian, pouting and looking at the ground where I left him.

"Who the fuck do you think I am, Bast? I'm not some whore who goes around flirting and fucking with people for the sake of it. *I'm your fucking wife,* and this…" I say while I point my hand between us, "is completely unacceptable. I have never given you a reason to doubt me. And I feel really offended right now."

If I'm being honest, he's looking at me with a seething look that scares me a lot. I have never seen him this worked up, and I don't know how he'll react. Bastian doesn't answer me and walks away. Turning his back to me, he heads into the shop where we rented our equipment for the day, leaving me alone, standing at the water's edge. My heart hammers so hard it causes a deafening silence around me.

What the actual fuck just happened? Everything was okay this morning. Why is this turning into a nightmare?

Deciding that I didn't have the time or patience to deal with Bastian's attitude, I launch the paddleboard into the water and take off on my own, wandering around the lake and exploring what nature has to offer. Anything to take my mind away from Bastian's odd wrath.

———

Pulling bendy, slender tree limbs out of my way, I follow the narrow tributary I found hidden. I slide along the water, allowing my paddleboard to slowly coast with the water's flow. I'm kneeling, looking around at the forest and taking in the various flora and foliage as I float. So far, I have cataloged over twenty species of native plants and four invasive types. I have even seen a variety of native butterflies that live in this area and a bright-green butterfly I have never seen before. It must be migrating through this area or it is really just a confused lunar moth who mixed up daytime and nighttime. Flowers and plants are my passion. It's why I chose to major in botany and, with Bastian's help, opened *Morning Glory Arrangements*, my first and very own florist shop.

I keep going back to what happened with Bastian earlier. This morning, everything was fine, maybe even better than fine. But now, I'm not so sure. I don't know how to quantify or measure Bastian's explosive anger. It threw me off balance, and now I'm trying to reclaim my Zen and peace of mind.

The caw of a red-shoulder crow catches my attention as he soars across the pickerel weeds and cardinal irises. As I follow his track and watch him glide closer to the water, I catch my reflection mirrored across the surface. I sigh to myself. I spent so much time getting ready, trying to look sexy, and damn, I do look good. I take a few moments to soak in my appearance.

My long strawberry-blond hair falls in perfect waves across my creamy, fair skin. The sun has darkened the freckles that brush across my cheeks and nose. You can see them in the water's reflection as they dot my nose and cheeks in a variety of constellations. Even my lips look fuller and red after this sunny exposure. Gazing deeper, I peer into my own emerald eyes, loving the thick, full curls of my eyelashes. I've never been vain, but even I can appreciate my natural beauty. Sometimes it just feels satisfying to relish in looking good. At five-five, I'm not overly skinny but have always been pleased with my curves. Taking a moment to brush my hair to the side as I admire my reflection, a shining strand draping across my shoulder catches my attention. I pick up an iridescent, delicate string.

When did I put this on?

Lifting the necklace away from my body, a pendant dangles at the end. So familiar, like I've seen it before. Holding the jewelry in my hand, I turn it around, feeling the rough edges and caressing the sharp edges. On the top of the pendant is a large, perfectly cut emerald that matches my eyes. Directly sitting under the stone is a round copper cage that contains a solitary black pearl.

Heavy and dainty, something about the pendant calls to my soul. *How do I know you*, I wonder. When I look deep into the emerald, red and yellow fire dances in the facets.

Suddenly, a face appears in my mind. Dark, onyx eyes filled with intensity and passion pierce my soul. I can almost feel his lips on mine. I can almost remember the warmth as he moves above me, bonding our souls forever. I tremble so hard I almost fall off my paddleboard. As I catch myself, my breathing is rapid. Slick wetness pours out of my sex.

Shaking my head and coming back to my senses, I look around. I'm leaning back on the paddleboard, clutching the sides for dear life. What the fuck was that? Did I just have an orgasm? I can feel sweat trickling down my forehead onto my chest as it rises and falls.

Before I process what just happened to me, Bastian comes around the corner, and panic is written all over his face as he yells. "ANNAAAA!!!! NOOO!!!!!!"

He's hurrying toward me so quickly that I cannot process his movements. When did he get that fast? I think I see him throw something my way, but I can't be sure of anything. My body is still recovering from the aftermath of whatever just happened. An invisible force knocks me from my paddle-board, lifting and slinging me into the air. I scream before I plunge into the dark water.

CHAPTER
Eight

JOLTING AWAKE, I'm shivering in terror. I was drowning, being pulled under by an unseen force. The remnants of the nightmare leave its evidence in sweat and tears. I wipe at my face and sit up, looking around to get myself oriented. All of a sudden, hands reach out and caress my arms. I jump, then scream at the touch. Looking to my right, I see the figure of a man.

"Livi, it's okay. It's just me, Jace. Are you okay, my morning glory?"

I see the outline of his face in the dark. His eyes are so dark that they look like miniature black holes, capturing all light. His hair is all messed up from sleep, or maybe my fingers tangling through his strands. There is worry etched along his forehead me waking him up from my drowning nightmare.

"I'm okay. I had a nightmare that I was drowning. It felt so weird. It felt real, Jace." Running my hands through my hair and holding my throat for a second, I'm still breathing very hard. My heart gallops so fast I think I might pass out.

Jace touches my face with the tips of his fingers. "Shhhhh,

it's okay, Livi love. You're safe here with me. It was just a dream. Besides, my beautiful, amazing mate, if I can help to ease your fears so you can sleep peacefully. Livi, my morning glory, you cannot drown."

"Huh?"

Jace reaches out to hold my hands—the familiar and repetitive gesture he uses when I feel upset. I'll admit, I love it, especially since he strokes the bottom of my palms with his fingers, igniting me internally. "Livi, since we bonded, our magic has been forged together. We cannot access all of our powers from each other, yet, because our union has not been blessed by the elders. We may only have a fraction of shared power right now but one thing I do know is you will never be able to drown. Water cannot harm you." He presses soft kisses to my knuckles while keeping my eyes connected to his.

Shaking my head, I stare at Jace in bewilderment. "That doesn't make any sense. I'm an Earth Fae, not a Water Fae like you, Jace, so how does being bonded to you prevent me from drowning? I should be as heavy as a rock and sink to the bottom."

"Exactly, Livi. You are Earth, and I'm Water. Just as the ocean tide can only caress the terrestrial shore and never submerge it forever, the water can touch you but not keep you under. The water, just as I do, loves you deeply. It will always protect you and keep you afloat. It was the first and strongest power gifted to you through our bond."

But rocks always sink to the bottom. I'm an Earth Fae, and geochemistry is one of my dominant powers. I know my power well; it's the understanding of Earth's formation, including the impacts of a substance's density. I reflect on our recent adventure and how I was able to create mud balls during our water shenanigans. I don't tell Jace this because there's no reason to dwell on the negatives, but something about the dream vexes me. I'm not sure what. But I forgot something…

I try to remember the dream, but I can't. The details are fuzzy, and the only thing I can recall with perfect clarity is the feeling of falling, then drowning. My throat is still sore from screaming in my dream. Was I screaming out loud in my sleep? I must have said that because Jace pulls me into his chest, wrapping his arms around me and nuzzling my neck.

Jace whispers into my ear, "It was only a bad dream, nothing more. I'm so glad you're awake. I know there is a natural progression of behaviors during the mating moon, but you have been sleeping a lot the past few days, and I've missed you." There is a small pout in his tone as he reaches around to grope my breast.

I laugh. "Really? I don't know, I just don't believe it." I contemplate what he said about sleeping so much lately but the thoughts are interrupted.

Jace grabs me by the waist and pulls me across his body to straddle his hips. I can feel his massive package resting under my own sex.

"Yes, really. It's one thing to enjoy fucking you into oblivion to help with the mating frenzy. Having you mentally present and ready to adventure is an entirely different feeling." He leans me over his face and kisses me so hard that I see stars. As he pulls away, he tells me, "Plus, it gives me hope."

"What kind of hope?"

Jace kisses me again and again before replying, "Hope that there is already life glowing within you."

His hands move to my stomach, and he spreads out his fingers. His eyes concentrate as if he has x-ray vision and can see something new and wonderful.

I tilt my head to the side and ask, "Well, is there?"

Jace sighs, the creases along his forehead relaxing as he

looks into my eyes. "Not sure just yet. I don't feel or detect anything."

Jace glances down. There is sadness in his tone, so I reach out, grab his chin, and force him to look back up at me.

"Hey, it's okay. If it doesn't happen during this heat, maybe my next one. We still have time right? This is just our first try."

I remembered that Jace told me my heat would last from new moon to new moon, and if I didn't get pregnant this time, we would have another chance next year when my body was primed and reset to try again.

"We do, and I know. I just thought that once it happened, I would, you know… just know. Our bodies are more than 70 percent water, and I had hoped I'd just feel it, sense new life growing in your brilliantly wonderful aquatic womb."

"Just because you can control water and determine what is in water doesn't mean that you can sense the moment we make a baby, Jace." I stroke his face, smiling at him. "Maybe you can, and we haven't yet, or maybe you can't, and we have. It's okay to find out the old-fashioned way." This means I just had to stop by our family physician, and he could take a urine sample to see if any hormones indicated we made a new life. He had potions that would change colors and indicate whether we were pregnant. Later on, he even has an alchemy set that can determine if we would have a boy or girl depending if the solution changed from green to blue or pink.

I lean down and press my lips to his. I only meant to give him a quick kiss, but Jace pulls me in closer, sliding his tongue across my bottom lip, urging me to open for him. I rock against his hardening length, our kiss becoming desperate, and my breathing labored.

Abruptly, I stop the kiss as I remember something I forgot and want to know. Looking at Jace, I ask him, "What happened on our wedding day?"

"Do you remember anything, Livi?"

Shaking my head, I tell him, "No, not really. Ever since you brought me to the cabin, my mind has been fuzzy. I remember feelings and a few things about myself, but everything else is just lost to me."

Sitting up in bed, Jace moves my body so we are snuggled and cuddling. "Hmm... sounds like symptoms of the mating haze. But you know what? Okay. I can do that. Come here. I would love to tell you the story of us."

Jace grants me one of his heart-stopping beautiful smiles. "I'll help you remember our dreams."

There's a mischievousness in his eyes as he starts his story.

"Once upon a time, there was a legend about a beautiful girl who met a very handsome boy"—Jace wiggles his eyebrows—"and the moment the boy saw the girl, he fell madly in love. You know, love at first sight and stuff."

I laugh at his silliness but find a much-needed comfort as I listen to his deep narrative.

Jace asks before continuing the story, "So you know that we have been mates since you were like born, and I was two, right? Some say in the Water Kingdom that the Earth quaked and the moon dipped down to see the birth of my mate. Of course I was still shitting in my diapers and crawling around the sandy floors of my parents' castle back then." Jace lets out a small laugh. "But the point is, we were fated mates even before creation."

I nod because I remember parts of this story but not everything. Jace can see this in my face and begins again.

"Yeah, so maybe I need to start somewhere near the beginning for this to make sense. I remember that every year, my mom brought me to your kingdom or your mom brought you to mine, and we had playdates. Once we started getting older, we would visit each other alone, hanging out and adventuring in either my parents' ocean castle or your parents' mountain chalet. We had a lot of time to get to know each other. We were each other's first kiss, our first touch." He says this while pulling my messy hair out of my face and bringing his mouth to mine. He gives me a gentle kiss before touching my face again.

"You are my first and only in all the senses of the word."

He kisses me again so tenderly that I melt in his arms. I feel so loved by him. This is a feeling I don't think I've had with anyone, and I never want it to go away. My only, my Jace, my mate.

He stops kissing me and sighs. "We have been planning our wedding for a long time... like I think about six years at this point. You kinda became obsessed about the time you finished Fae academy and I was serving in the Fae militia for the water realm. We built this cabin in the woods to have privacy because you were too loud when I fucked you during deployment reprieves. I have to admit my selfishness and jealousy issues, I didn't want anyone hearing you scream. Your ecstasy is mine and only mine. Always has been, always will be."

I laugh at this. I have to give it to him. I'm really loud, so I understand him not wanting anyone to hear me when I'm yelling his name and asking him to give it to me harder. I reflect on the few times he was able to sneak into my dorms at the academy. I'm pretty sure my roommate and BFF Milly, really hated me during those sleepless nights.

He laughs with me and continues with our story that I don't recall for some reason. I can remember a few details but not all of it. Maybe it's the mating moon and hormonal haze, but I really want to know our entire story.

"Our wedding day," Jace starts, then continues.

"I thought it was perfect. Even though guests had to travel, we knew we wanted a destination wedding. We had the mountain chapel that is three days south of your parents castle filled with your favorite flowers, bouquets and garlands made of pink and yellow tulips, orange sunflowers, blue and purple hydrangeas, and roses in every color. It was a damn kaleidoscope. Fairy lights twinkled around the ceiling and room, casting a warm, inviting glow so our guests could see everything. We went with an early afternoon wedding but used heavy, light-blocking curtains to make the chapel feel intimate. Everything was exactly what we wanted, from the tiniest details to the grandest adornments.

"The room had this energy that everyone could feel, and it was magic. I was at the front waiting for you. I knew you would look beautiful in your dark-green wedding dress. I know I wasn't supposed to know, but I couldn't help myself. When you were getting ready with your mom and Milly, I snuck a peek. You were breathless and stunning, and I was trying to prepare myself to see you again and not cry like a baby." I smile softly at him because I can see his love for me while he recounts what happened last week.

"I wore the tux you selected but decided to go with the black tie. I know you wanted the dark green to match your dress, but I just couldn't do it. I needed to look all dark and handsome for you. I needed to look all me." Jace emphasizes, "I added the black and gray opals with the green tea rose boutonnieres to my tux, adding the matching element of our love of the earth and oceans. If I say so, I looked damn good that day.

"So there I was in the front, waiting for you. But the time passed, and you never showed up. I started getting anxious and went to look for you. I asked your mom to see why you were taking so long, but she told me that you were ready and that she just left you in the room to wait for your dad. That's when your dad came running toward us and said the bridal suite was empty. I panicked and ran to the room. When I got there, you weren't there. Everything was in perfect order in the room, but you were missing. So we called the guards and started looking for you. In the pit of my stomach, I felt and just knew that something was not right."

I can't believe what I'm hearing. Why would I disappear if we wanted to get married? And to Jace, my mate? My forever... this doesn't make sense.

"We looked everywhere in the castle. Even the guests started helping. Your mom was a mess and could not stop crying, but I knew something bad happened to you."

"So what happened next? How did I wake up here in bed? How long was I missing?" I have so many questions, and I need the answers.

Jace passes his hand through his hair, releasing a frustrated sound, and continues.

"Thirty-six hours. That's how long it took for me to find you. Thirty-six of the longest fucking hours of my life."

"Where was I? How did you find me?"

"I found you running through the swamp, making a beeline for our cabin. At first, I was hopeful and excited, but the closer I got to you, the faster you ran from me. It was as if your heat had already taken over, and you relied on your basal Fae instincts. I can remember looking at your face and seeing your eyes glazed over like you were in a trance. When I finally caught you, you freaked out and screamed before fainting. So I did what I thought was best and brought you here, to our home.

"While you recovered, I reached out to our families. Your mom wants to see you, but mine keeps telling her not to worry. That this is part of the natural way, and we need to be left alone until this mating haze ends. So I've done what is expected and desired. I have loved you and your body as you have needed."

I stare at Jace, processing his words. "That's a lot to digest, Jace," I tell him quietly. "It just seems so..."

"I know, Liv. I feel the same way. We'd prepared for a heightened mating moon, but this doesn't make sense to me either. But I promise we'll figure it out together. Come on, I want to take you somewhere. I think it might help with your memories."

———

The forest is less dense here. Light filters down through the canopy onto the fallen leaves that cover the still frozen ground. Jace holds my hand in his as he pulls me along an old forgotten pathway, guiding me through the fog that is slowly burning away. The trickling of a creek can be heard not too far ahead. A few birds chirp on the naked branches, singing for Spring and warmer weather.

"We are almost there," Jace tells me as he pulls back a heavy tree branch hanging across the trail.

Sitting alone in a clearing is an ancient, copper-colored rustic forge. An anvil sits to the side, the black paint faded to gray and brown. Pieces of the cast iron flake away, dusting the ground around it.

"What is this place?" I ask Jace as we walk up to the structure. I can see that the furnace was used recently. Hammers, tongs, and other forging tools are lying around.

Not too far away is the creek I heard, a small spring bubbling water up from the ground. A bucket sits nearby for transporting water. Smart, some blacksmith built The Forge near a natural water source, making curing and tempering easier.

"This place is known as The Fabricate. This fable goes that centuries ago, a blacksmith on the hunt for water was following the sounds of the spring. In his desperation to mitigate his thirst, when he finally found where the water breached the surface, he barreled over a sunbathing tree nymph, knocking her from her slumber. Falling to the ground, he rolled over and expected to experience a fury and violence like none other since he pulled her from her nap.

However, the moment they looked into each other's eyes, it was fate. They were mates. Her rage evaporated faster than the dew on a hot summer morning.

"At that moment of calmness, The Forge appeared out of nowhere as our blacksmith helped his lady nymph from where she lay. Together, they took the appearance of The Forge as a sign and built their home, having many children and using The Forge to create whatever they needed to survive. Through their love, this area was infused with magic to wield anything. Now, many centuries later, The Fabricate is still here, ready to forge for whoever is in need of binding materials together."

As Jace tells me this story, he's walking me around the area. I can almost imagine a burly, big man running through the woods and tripping over a lovely nymph, just minding her own business. I'm smiling as I imagine them building their home and having their babies. Making love right here on the leaves of the forest floor.

I can feel the love and the magic. It radiates through the atmosphere, permeating into the ground. A memory briefly assaults me. A first time, a penetration, a quick pain, then pleasure like I have never known before.

"Jace. I have been here before. Something feels… familiar."

"You have, Liv. Several times. We used to come out here and play, hide, climb trees, be kids, become one for the first time. Be us."

"It's so surreal. I can feel their history, and if I close my eyes, I can almost see them here. Why do you think their love created The Forge?"

"I don't know if their love created The Forge, per se, but I know through their love they could create and weld anything they wanted. It was thought that they could force rare earth metals together and harness the magic as well as even change the magic for what they needed."

Wow, that's really cool. "Have we ever forged anything here?" I ask Jace. Slightly blushing as another memory of moving bodies, panting in ecstasy, pushes its way into my mind.

"Why yes, my Livi, many things." Jace smiles as he pulls me to him and brushes hair off my shoulder. Instead of touching me, though, Jace picks up the necklace around my neck, holding the pendant in his hands.

"This, my love, we forged this necklace for you here"—Jace dangles the pendant now—"and this ring, for me." Jace pulls a ring off his left fourth finger. It's a perfect complement to my necklace except instead of one pearl and one emerald, it's a repeating pattern of small pearls and emeralds. "These stones allow us to share our power. It's how I know that no matter what, you can never drown. The magic won't let it happen. And if you were to sink under for some outlandish reason, I would know, and I would be there to protect you and help you rise above the waves." Jace's lips meet mine, and he kisses me like I'm his queen, like I'm the other half of his soul. I return the kiss with the same energy and fervent need because he's my other half. As we clutch the pendant between our hands, the world contracts and expands, orgasmically exploding as our powers intertwine, circling us in a protective embrace.

As Jace lays me down among the cold leaves, his lips leave mine long enough to whisper in my ear, "And this my love, is where I claimed you as mine for the very first time."

Jace's lips reclaim mine as he slides his right arm under my dress, his fingers caress me along my inner thigh. Heat spreads through my body, filling me from my core to my finger tips. Jace uses his other hand to pull my dress up and over my head, leaving me exposed, completely bare to nature. I feel my Earth power sparking to life. I squeeze my palms into the ground as a rush of magic leaves my body. Cushioned moss springs up around us with wild violets blanketing the cool Earth.

"There's my Earth Princess," Jace says in between kisses. "I love it when you allow your magic to flow with nature."

Jace captures my right breast in his mouth before he rises to his knees, releasing my nipple with an audible pop. Blue fire dances in his hungry black eyes. He quickly removes his clothes, leaving his impressive length standing upright against his stomach. A gasp leaves my throat. Stars he is so hard and long. I just want to lean up and lick the drop of pre-cum I see glistening on the head of his shaft but Jace pushed my shoulders back to the ground.

Jace moves to lay his body between my legs. With every heartbeat, I can feel the pulse of the Earth, I can feel the tremors of the rocks moving as continents shift. "Jace," I whisper as his hands touch everywhere. I feel worshipped, cherished as he presses kisses down my neck, along my chest, across my belly.

Thorned vines have started growing up the trees that surround us with bright pink and burnt orange flower blossoms. Snow drifts softly downward covering us in a thin sheet of moisture, attempting to cool our molten bodies. The world has fallen quiet except for the sounds of my breathy pleas.

"Please Jace… I need.."

"Shh my Livi, I know what you need, let me love you." Jace steals my breath and voice as his lips latch onto my clit without warning. The orgasm screams through my body. I wasn't ready for it, but now I want more, I need more. I scream Jace's name at the top of my lungs as he pushes two fingers inside. My back arches from the forest floor. Tulips and narcissist burst from the ground as Jace praises me, telling me, "Stars Liv, you are so fucking wet. Come for me again my love, come again."

I come two more times on Jace's tongue and fingers before

he finally stops. His face is glistening with my pleasure as he drags his body back up mine. When he kisses me all I taste is an explosion of strawberries, mint, and sunflower? The flavors burst in my mouth as Jace devours me and our tongues duel. "I could feast on you all day my love, you taste divine."

My entire sex is swollen, sensitive, but I need so much more. I wrap my legs around Jace's lower back, inching him closer to where I need him. "Jace...," I start to beg, but my mate knows me and my body. In a powerful surge, Jace thrusts into me, burying his cock to the hilt. We both release a moan as our bodies finally connect to become one entity. With his forehead against mine, Jace begins to move, sliding in and out of me slowly at first, then picking up speed.

"Livi...," he says my name like it's a benediction. My nails dig into his back, massaging his muscles as he begins to truly pound me into the ground. Our gaze has remained locked and I am captivated by the fires burning in his eyes. Sapphire and cyan flames are the only indication that Jace has some Fire Fae genetics in his ancestry. I can feel his water powers building, wanting to play with my Earth magic.

Jace grabs onto the back of my thighs, pushing them apart as he lifts us in a new position. Holding me upwards, Jace slams into me, harder and harder. I am a panting, moaning mess as he reaches between us and starts circling my clit with his thumb. A force I cannot see begins to tumble and crash through us. Like a plunging wave, the orgasms breaks with so much energy that magic spills out of us both as we find our release together. I'm chanting Jace's name like a prayer, over and over as the energy continues to crest over us, pulling us into another oceans of orgasms as we float along a river of pleasure. I look upwards, the forest now a cacophony of color and life.

My heart pounds, perfectly synchronized with Jace's own cardiac rhythm. Each beat tugging at the eternal mate bond

Jace and I share as he, still rock hard, begins to slowly glide within me again, Within a few precious moment, Jace sends us cascading over the edge once again. Our names but a melodic breeze in the wind as they escape our now raspy voices.

CHAPTER
Nine

WHEN I OPEN MY EYES, I can see the gentle light of the sun coming through my window, acknowledging the presence of morning. I sigh and stretch. I'm considering if I should go back to sleep. That was the best rest ever. I feel so cozy in this bed. I close my eyes and think about what happened yesterday with Jace and how he made me feel. How the dance of our combined powers made me feel so invigorated. Bless, he's so handsome, and every time I look at him, I get fluttering butterflies in my stomach. I wonder if that will stop in the future or if I will still feel the same in thirty or three hundred years from now. He makes me feel like I can conquer the world. He also makes me feel beautiful, cherished, desired, wanted, and unique. He makes me feel eternal, infinite love.

I still can't believe that I'm a Fae, and he's my mate, the missing half of my soul. How amazing! I turn around to hug Jace.

My bed is empty. Desolate. Cold on the side that should contain my…

I open my eyes and realize I'm not in our cabin. I'm in my house. The house that I share with… my husband.

Bastian.

I look around and see the same white walls and the same rusty peach-colored drapes on my windows. How is it that when I opened my eyes a few minutes ago, I didn't realize I was not in the cabin? That dream with Jace felt so real. His touch, the way I feel when he's nearby. That understanding of completion that surrounds me when I'm near him. I have never felt that with Bastian. I know Jace in my soul... but... who is Bastian?

I feel so fucking confused right now. *How can a dream be so vivid? How is it that I can remember every detail of my dream? How can I still feel Jace's lips on mine, his body wrapped with mine? How can I still smell the lingering scents of woodsy spice and salty ocean? Fuck, I can still taste him on my tongue. Is this dream real, or just a figment of my fucked-up imagination?*

I want to cry. I'm so confused and upset. Frustration builds throughout my body. I scream and bang my hands into the covers over and over again. I want to rip and tear them up. I need to go back there. I need to get back to Jace. There's no way that was just a dream. It felt too real... It felt... too much. A heavy need emboldens me to make a decision: I must go back.

Jumping out of bed, I run to the bathroom. Seeing my reflection, I almost scream again. It should be because I'm naked. I don't remember putting on my pajamas. But no, that is not what startles me, scares me.

The pendant Jace and I forged at The Fabricate before our bonding ceremony is attached to a delicate, iridescent chain between my breasts.

How can I have this pendant in my life when Jace is just a dream? This is so wrong. This must mean something if I can have this pendant.

I'm struggling to breathe as panic sets in. I have to think, slow down. I need to see if Bastian gave me this necklace at some point in our marriage, or if I bought it and that's why I dreamed of it. There must be an explanation of why I'm wearing this pendant.

I grab the pendant and really look at it. It feels warm in my hands.

That's when I remember… A fire in a cabin. Strong arms holding me. Playing in the water. Exploring the lake when I was alone on my paddleboard and cataloging. I crashed into the water. I remember it now… Bastian yelled my name and waved his hands at me before a force pushed me toward the water. But what happened after that? Because I just remember that I woke up next to Jace, and we talked about my dream. But was that it… my head spins. My realities are twisted, and I cannot figure out which is mine. They're confusing me, blending in their realness.

How the fuck am I in this house when I feel that my real life is with Jace? I think I'm going positively mad. I look at myself in the mirror. I can see my chest rise and fall with each rapid breath. I feel this weight in my chest. I think I'm drowning in a panic attack.

The air is leaving my lungs, but I can't seem to take a breath in. Oh my goodness, the edges of my vision are going dark, and I think I'm going to faint. I can't stop looking at the pendant in my hands. I feel clammy, but the jewel burns my palm.

"Breathe, Ana, just breathe," I tell myself.

Then I start to count from one to ten over and over again.

I grab the corners of the counter and press really hard and count. "One, two, three, four…"

Closing my eyes, I imagine Jace's face. That's when my panic slows. I just keep focusing on his beautiful face, those full lips, his thick black hair. I imagine his smile and the way I feel every time he gifts me with it. I think about his beautiful tattoos that cover the top part of his pecs, the lighthouse, calling me home. His strong arms embrace me, protecting me. Last, I think about his beautiful dark eyes. Those onyx eyes that capture me and hold me hostage. I can't escape from this feeling. I need to hold on to this feeling. To this memory. "Livi…" The whisper of his voice ghosts across my lips.

When I open my eyes and look at myself again, I'm breathing normally. I'm determined to go back to Jace. He must be real. That had to have been real.

My life with him feels more real every time I think of it. I wash my face and brush my teeth. Changing out of my pajamas, I pull on some shorts and a shirt. Then I start looking around the house for Bastian.

Where is he? Now that I'm thinking clearly, I really need to talk to him.

Why can't I remember getting out of the lake and coming home? How is it possible that I feel that I'm going crazy? Why can I remember more about the necklace and Jace than how I returned to my bedroom?

I look in the living room, and everything is clean and in order, but no Bastian. I see a picture beside the TV. Curious, I walk over and grab it. It's a picture of Bastian and me on our wedding day. I'm wearing a simple, a-line white dress. The crown of my hair is held back with a white lily attached to a cathedral veil as my long, strawberry waves are left loose, cascading down my breasts and back.

In the picture, I look at Bastian with adoration on my face, and Bastian looks at the camera. He's wearing a white tux with a white shirt and a blush rose cumberbund. In the background is a beautiful arch of white flowers, daisies, impatiens, gladiolas, gardenias, and hyacinths. All white.

I can't stop looking at this picture. I question why in the world is there so much white? I thought I didn't want any white at the wedding. I wanted every color. And why lilies? My favorites are tulips, roses, sunflowers, zinnias… this doesn't make any sense.

I have no recollection of this day. This does not look like a wedding I would want. I'm looking at Bastian, and I feel content, but it is nothing compared to what I feel with Jace. Just imagining him causes shivers to run up my spine.

I return the picture and turn around to walk to the kitchen. On the counter is a covered plate with a sticky note on it.

I made you breakfast, sweetheart. Enjoy. I'll miss you until I see you in a couple of days when I come back from my conference.
Love, - B

Moving the napkin from the plate, I see French toast covered with powdered sugar. Fruit and a warmed ramekin of maple syrup are on the side. My stomach growls, so I decide to eat. I can't think straight with an empty stomach. I indulge and eat, filling my hungry belly.

After finishing my breakfast, I venture to each room in the house, but nothing I could see told me this was my house. Everything looks so generic. If this was my house, I would have put vivid colors on the wall, and I would have so many flowers.

How is it that I have a flower shop and don't have flowers in my house?

I go outside to the back patio and, again, find no signs of flowers or a garden. Just grass… This doesn't make any sense to me at all. I need to go back to sleep. I'm not where I'm supposed to be. This isn't right. I need to see Jace.

I'm not sure what to do, but at least I know Bastian won't be here for the next few days.

Running back into my bedroom, I go straight to my medicine cabinet. I don't know why, but I know I have to go back to sleep. I need to try to find my way back to whatever dream has Jace.

Grabbing a full bottle of Benadryl, I only take a moment to

pause and reflect on the decision I'm about to make. If I take one, I know I will be drowsy. Two will definitely put me to sleep, but for how long? Deciding that three should be enough to knock me out without being fatal and causing me to overdose, I throw my head back and drink down the pills.

Then I crawl into my bed, cover myself, and wait for sleep to take me back to Jace.

CHAPTER

Ten

MY EYELIDS FEEL HEAVY, and my jaws stretch in a wide yawn. I just want to go back to sleep. Everything is so peaceful in my dreams. No real world to stress you out or lay unwelcome expectations. Stretching my back and arms, I try to think about what needs to be done for the day at the shop.

Going over the list in my head, I begin to plan out the pre-ordered flower arrangements and wonder if I have enough supplies for any last-minute orders.

"Does Janet work today?" I ask myself.

Turning over, I snuggle into the covers and take one deep breath.

"Wait." I pause. I push my nose into the pillow beside mine and breathe again. Deeper this time.

Rainy woods, musky amber, salty ocean. I sigh deeply and think of one name who owns this personalized fragrance.

Jace.

I bolt to my feet as the memories rush back. The Benadryl! I swallowed those three pills. *Fuck.... holy... what in the Fae world. I'm back, just wow...* I'm breathless.

The cabin is dark, but I can still make out enough of my

surroundings to know that I did it. I made it back to the Fae Realm. I made it home to Jace. My Jace.

My heart throbs. I quickly walk over to the curtains near the bed and open them. Morning light filters in through a foggy haze. I walk around the cabin and open all of the curtains.

"Where is my mate?" I question myself. He's not in the cabin. I need to find him and tell him about these dreams. This has to be more than just symptoms of a mating haze. Something's not right. He needs to know...

Throwing on a robe that I found hanging on the bathroom door, I pull on some slippers and walk out the front door to the cabin. Out here, the fog looks thicker, and I can barely see the trees ten feet away.

Looking around, I don't see Jace. I decide to walk around the cabin because maybe he's out back. But I don't find him there either. Finally, I call out. Maybe I can't see him through the fog, but he can hear me.

"Jace! Jace... Where are you?"

Making my way carefully around the cabin, I continue calling out for my mate.

"JACE!"

Jace is nowhere to be seen as I make my way back to the front door. I'm starting to get scared. A chill sends shivers up my spine, yet there is no breeze in the air. Looking out to the tree edge, I feel as if someone or something is watching me. Paranoid, I scurry back inside the cabin and lock the front door.

I need to find Jace, but at the same time, I don't remember my way around the forest, and I don't want to get lost in the fog. I'm starting to get scared and for more than one reason. What if I'm dreaming, and I fucked up? What if taking that Benadryl was a horrible idea... I really hope I didn't over-dose. Panicking, I rummage through every drawer and cabinet in the cabin. Towels, clothes, more blankets, and food supplies get littered around the cabin as I hurl things. I'm not sure what I'm looking for, but I know there must be something in this cabin that can explain things.

Sitting on my bottom, I shove myself away from the chest of drawers next to the bed. I sigh in frustration. What am I missing?

I fall on my back, staring up at the ceiling. I just want to kick and scream. However, before I can throw a tantrum, a glimmer from under the bed grabs my attention.

Huh, I wonder, *what is that?*

I rotate and crawl under the bed as far as I can, grabbing a rather large box and pulling it to me.

It's a memory box. Jackpot! This is what I've been searching for... this box has to have all of my answers.

I open the lid and sitting on top of a pile of letters is a conch seashell, several feathers, a compass, and a dried red rose, thorny stem still attached. Lifting the items one at a time, I gingerly rotate each in my hands. The conch seashell is big enough to run my index finger along the inside ridge. Wondering if the rumors are true, I hold the shell to my ear and listen.

Sure enough, I can hear ocean waves crashing on a shoreline. I swear I hear a seagull laughing in the breeze. My eyes open wide at my surprise. Setting the shell down, I move to the feathers. There's a variety of them, all colors of reds, blues, greens, grays. Some are from shorebirds, the others from songbirds here in the forest. I arrange the feathers in a colorful order and lay them to the side. Next, I pick up the rose, just a single dried red rose. I wonder when Jace gave me this, or maybe I gave it to him. There's an inkling of a memory trying to break free as I rub my fingers across the velvety, dry petals. Something about growing a rose garden for his mom years ago...

Last, I pick up the compass. The piece is set in copper; it's hefty and the size of my palm. Popping open the lid, I read the inscription:

For always finding your way North.
- Love, O.

Without warning, a vision flickers to the front of my mind. It's of me, giving the compass to Jace. I remember how I used to get so upset when Jace would have to travel the southern shores with the coast guard back home to his parents' castle or even farther to the southern countries that can only be accessed by boat. He would always tell me that I was his northern lights, that I shone so brightly I could guide him back home from the darkest places. During that time I went through a phase signing all my letters to him with my first initial.

I can't believe I forgot that. I would joke and tell him that he was my lighthouse. Always safely guiding me home. Then we would dissolve into a fit of giggles and stolen kisses. How old were we then? I think I was fourteen, maybe fifteen since he began his enlistment time early.

I put the compass to the side with the rest of the artifacts and pick up the top letter written in an elegant script. The seal has already been popped. Turning it around so that I can read, I realize that the letter is in a Fae language. Odd. Should I know how to read this? The characters are shapes that seem familiar, but I'm having trouble deciphering the message. Flipping the paper around, I look to see if there is a key or code on the back. Maybe we have our own language like pig latin, and I just have to figure it out. However, I have no luck in finding a code or clue for understanding what I'm looking at. I put the letter down and dig through the rest of the box, trying to find something I can read.

I go through letter after letter. They are all in the same

bizarre language, but I notice two distinct types of handwriting. One scrawl is long, smooth, and elegant. The other is blocked and neat. Without understanding the writing, I can guess who wrote which letters. The only thing I recognize is the format of the letter and what may be the dates each letter was written. If I'm correct in my assumptions, these letters go back more than a decade. As I reach the bottom of the box, if the dates are accurate, the first letter was written when I may have been eight or nine years old. The memory box contains hundreds of letters on various types of parchment. Some are long, and others are short. What I would give to be able to read just one.

As if knowing what I need, the words on the letter in my hand rearrange themselves. It's magic! Changing from the strange characters to an alphabet that I know, sentences reframe and restructure. I'm so shocked that I almost drop the letter. But it's the first line that keeps the paper in my grips.

It's the dreams we will build together that will become our happiest reality.

Lightning cracks outside the cabin, ripping my focus from the letter. I scream in fright as thunder shakes the walls, and the letter floats to the floor.

Where in the world is Jace? He should have shown up by now if he left the cabin for some reason.

Another bolt of lightning illuminates the room. It's starting to storm outside. I go to stand from the nest of stuff I have scattered on the floor and almost immediately lose my balance. My head swims, and I feel like I have a bit of vertigo. I carefully make my way to the bed, holding on to the edges of the mattress. My head spins faster. I can hear the rain pounding on the roof. A thudding migraine forms at the back of my head.

Jace, I must find him. He can help me; he can fix this.

Somehow I stumble my way to the front door and sling it open. Screaming as loud as I can into the storm, I call for my mate, "JACE!!!!!!"

Strong winds whip my hair around my face. Raindrops feel like fire and ice as they pelt my skin. Something is wrong; I can feel it within my core. I know Jace is out there somewhere, and I need to go find him. Stepping away from the entry, I only take a few more seconds to make my decision. I cannot stay here any longer. If Jace is not coming to me, he must be in trouble, so I need to go to him. I shake my head to clear away some of the fuzziness from the impending headache and then run out the door.

Within a few steps outside, I'm already soaked and fighting to see through the sheets of rain. Where would Jace be? What would Jace do? There's so much water around me that, for a moment, I'm afraid I could drown standing up. I remember Jace telling me that water is my friend, and I can now control it, too.

Reaching deep inside, I feel for my powers. It's a tiny spark, but I know I'm doing something right. Imagining an umbrella, I hold my hands above my head, pointing my palms upward. The rain begins to slosh away from me. I'm controlling an invisible force shielding me from the downfall. Something calls from deep within me, and I answer.

A bright-green light radiates from inside me. I can feel a familiar power surging through me. This is mine, intimately, recognizably mine. It's steady and strong, with an undercurrent of Jace's water magic.

Fueling my desire to find Jace, I allow the magic to surround me, creating a protective bubble from the torrent of rain. Visibility is worse now than earlier in the fog, and I have to decide on my direction. Something heavy in my pocket bangs against my leg. Sticking my hand in my pocket, I pull out the compass. *When did I grab this?*

I open the compass, and the needle glows, pointing toward true north. Jace, he must be there. I break out into a run, skirting through trees, dodging limbs and other brush. I keep glancing down at the compass, and the farther I travel, the brighter the needle glows. Hopefully, this means I'm on the right path and not too far from Jace.

Abruptly, I come to the edge of a cliff. I have to stop so quickly that I give myself whiplash. In this weather, I cannot see how far down the drop goes, but the needle is still glowing and pointing in the direction of the abyss. I know I need to keep going forward in order to find Jace.

A loud snapping sound from behind me catches my attention. At first, I think it's a tree limb that has cracked in the storm. I'm not prepared for the beast rising up on its haunches. At least ten feet tall, it opens its mouth to expose long, serrated teeth. Stunned, I try to remain as still as possible, hoping it cannot see me in this rain.

Orange, snake-like eyes are my only clue that I've been noticed. The creature roars at me, drawing its body up taller and stalking, no slithering toward me!

I can't go backward, and I definitely can't run forward. Fuckity fuck fuck. Glancing over my shoulder, I realize that backward may be my only escape option.

Closer now, I can smell rot and mildew coming off the monster. I have to be quick, or it's going to get me. My heart pounds, and my legs shake. I may be about to make a really bad decision. Turning around, I run and throw myself over the ledge. I'm not fast enough, and the creature's fangs graze my back.

Rain drives sharply into my skin as I try to call my powers back to shield me from the monsoon, but they are gone, completely disappeared. Blinding-hot pain ricochets throughout my body. I scream and scream as I begin to plummet. I try to call for my powers again but get nothing in return.

Free-falling, I put all my energy into one last cry, pleading for the only one who can rescue me. "JACE!" The sound of my voice echoes hauntingly off the cliff walls as the black abyss swallows me whole.

CHAPTER
Eleven

THE WORST NIGHTMARE I have had in several nights disturbs my sleep. My heart thumps as I collect my bearings. I was falling, then darkness. I'm still disoriented, so I keep my eyes closed.

Waking up slowly, I realize I feel all warm and cozy.

Yawning, I turn in bed, looking for Jace. I want to feel his body next to mine. His lips next to my lips. When I find him, I snuggle deep into his warmth. The hard feel of his muscles is very appealing, so I start stroking his arms and snuggle closer to his neck. He feels good but different. Inhaling, I realize he smells different, too. Lavender and frankincense, like the soap I brought back from the monastery when hunting for a specific type of flower for the Owen's family dinner last Christmas.

Huh. Where did that thought come from, I wonder.

I'm about to open my eyes when I hear him take in a deep breath before he pulls me closer against him and his hard-ening length. This forces me to burrow my head further into his neck.

"Good morning, sweetheart."

My eyes open suddenly, and I see that it's Bastian, who

I'm hugging and snuggling. I'm so fucking confused. Was I not with Jace at the cabin last night? I thought I was no longer here and went back there. These dreams of mine are messing with my mind. I don't know what is real anymore. I'm stuck.

But this man, my husband who is beside me, feels real right now. So what the hell?

I need to stop thinking about these dreams. They are so lucid, and while they seem amazing, they confuse my reality. I feel sad one moment, and I'm also extremely tired the next. It's like every time I'm in a dream, I use all my energy.

This needs to stop today. I need to get my head right and figure out why I'm having lingering effects on my brain after the accident.

I can probably talk to Janet about this, or better yet, I can make an appointment with a therapist. If I talk to Janet about this, she won't understand and would think it's okay because they are just dreams. I need a professional's opinion. Definitely not Bastian's since I'm dreaming about another man who gives great orgasms...

No, not a good idea. But maybe he knows someone. This is not right, and I need to get my head straight.

I want to vent and rant and get this off my chest. I need to think about Bastian. How would he feel if he knew I was thinking about another man who is not even real? Yet all these dreams that I'm having about Jace and his world seem so real and feel so right when I'm there. How can I explain this weirdness?

Shaking my head back and forth, I decide I'm over-thinking things. Dreams are just dreams, and I must be crazy to think a dream could be real.

With my mind made up that I'm where I'm supposed to be and that this is the real world, I roll over to look at Bastian and smile. "Good morning, husband. How did you sleep? How were your travels? What time did your plane land? I don't remember you coming home or joining me in the bed at all."

Bastian kisses my forehead. "It was okay. Travel was fine. I'm glad the conference is over, and I'm home. But I know one thing that would have helped me sleep better," he murmurs in my ear before placing a kiss right below it.

"And what would that have been?" I breathily ask him.

"If I had you the way I wanted you last night."

"Oh really? Well, then why didn't you wake me up when you got home?" I ask.

Now I'm very curious. Didn't we talk about this already? I told him to wake me up whenever he wanted me, no matter what time he got home.

"I tried waking you up with kisses. I caressed you all over your body, but you were not responding. So I thought to myself, my baby is tired, and she's had a rough few months since the accident. I decided to let you sleep and just hold you in my arms."

That's when I remembered the Benadryl. Fuck, I'm losing it. Did I really take some Benadryl to force myself to go to sleep and see Jace? Well, that didn't fucking work, did it? I just had the nightmare of nightmares. No wonder Bastian couldn't wake me up with his loving attentions.

Plus, I can't tell Bastian about the pills because he'll think I'm crazy. What husband wants to know that his wife is taking medicine to see her dream man? He'll have me committed if I admit to taking medicine just to go back into a dream. The fact he's a therapist just makes this situation so much worse.

"Well, I guess if you want me, then you better do something about it right now." I wiggle my eyebrows, trying to change the mood. I quickly jump from the bed before Bastian can grab me. "But first, let me brush my teeth, please."

I don't want him to smell my dragon breath this early in the morning. I must have snored because it's rank. Plus, I always hate it when I read books or watch movies of people waking up and immediately start kissing and fucking. I need to be kissed if I'm having sex. But there is no way I will feel aroused with this stinky breath.

Bastian reaches out for me, trying to tug me back to the bed. "Let me be clear, I don't care about your breath. I'll kiss your dragon mouth. But, sure, if that makes you happy, then, yes, let's brush our teeth."

I move from the bed, and as I'm passing Bastian, he slaps my ass hard and winks. "Now, hurry up, baby. I want breakfast, and I know exactly what I'm hungry for this morning."

I giggle, knowing exactly what he likes to feast on, and walk faster to the bathroom where I proceed to do my business and brush my teeth. Bastian stands next to me, done with his morning routine, giving me predatory glances. He puts his arms around me pulling me close as he leans down. He tortures and teases me by kissing up and down my neck while I'm trying to finish my own routine.

I feign impatience, but let's be real, I love when he does this. I get very hot and bothered when he kisses the back of my neck, especially near my ears. Then when he nips, I shiver and step away to finish.

Once I'm done, Bastian doesn't hesitate as he turns me around and kisses me like a man starved. I guess he really did miss me. I'm so wet from all the kissing. He has me so worked up that I can't wait to have him inside me.

He wraps his arms around my sides and pulls my shirt over my head. I help him take it the rest of the way off before our lips fight for control. Between bruising kisses, Bastian moves his hands down my ass and pulls my panties off my legs. He kneels. He grabs my hips and pulls me to trace kisses along my thighs. When he reaches my core, Bastian pauses, then takes a deep breath and smells me. He looks up at me and just smiles. "Delicious," he mutters before standing and grabbing me by the ass so he can place me on top of the counter.

Bastian stands between my legs and looks at me with so much desire that it's making me dripping wet. A mischievous smile crosses his face as he states, "I'm going to have my breakfast now."

Agonizingly slow, Bastian places kisses down my body. His lips circle the nipple of my right breast while he pinches my other. I moan with pleasure. My breathing is getting erratic. I'm feeling impatient. I can't wait for him to go down on me. He keeps going south, planting open-mouthed kisses along my stomach before he grabs my thighs and spreads my legs farther apart. Bastian stares down at my soaking wet pussy with fascination in his eyes. He looks up at me with his bright-blue eyes before asking, "Are you ready, baby?"

"Yes, Bastian. Please…"

He doesn't let me finish talking as he pulls me toward the edge of the counter and buries his head between my legs. He starts kissing my core, licking me from ass to clit. His tongue flattens and focuses on my hard nub. I'm dying with pleasure.

"So fucking sweet. I can't get enough," Bastian says between kisses.

I grab Bastian's head and pull him closer to my clenching pussy. Tangling my fingers in his hair, I tug him until he consumes me. He sucks hard on my clit and moves one of his fingers to my center. He starts pumping his finger in and out, sucking my clit at the same time. The rhythm feels like I'm dancing in heaven.

His lips suction onto my clit so tightly I almost come, flying off the counter. Bastian adds a second finger alongside the first. Gripping the edge of the counter for my life, I'm enthralled watching him eat me out. I can hear the wet sound of my sex as I clench his fingers again and again. I'm so close to my release, but I need more. I move my hips at the same pace as his fingers, seeking the desperately needed friction.

I beg him. "I need more, please, more." I'm practically crying for him.

Bastian moves one of his free fingers to massage the tight ring around my asshole. I have never been fucked in the ass, but the way it feels right now, I bet you anything that I can get on board with it. It's a slow process, but once he has a whole finger inside my ass, he adds his other two in my pussy, and I'm a goner.

I come so hard. I don't know what I'm screaming; I just know I feel raw and alive. Bastian doesn't stop sucking my clit until I stop trembling from the aftershocks of my orgasm. My clit is getting very sensitive. I want to jump from the slightest contact.

Bastian looks at me. His face is wet with my arousal. Licking his lips, he tells me, "Damn, that's the best breakfast ever, Ana."

I'm still breathing hard and coming down from my climax when he grabs me by the hips and helps me down from the counter. He kisses me deeply, and I taste myself on his tongue. It turns me on so much more, I squeeze my thighs together.

Bastian grabs my face and moves his mouth to my neck and sucks hard. I sigh because I like what he's doing. I don't think I'll mind a little hickey bruising.

Suddenly, Bastian turns me around and looks at my reflection in the mirror. He bends me over the counter and smacks my right ass cheek hard before he gently massages the area.

"You are so fucking beautiful. Your ass looks so beautiful with my handprint on it." He spanks my ass again on the other cheek. Slickness is pouring out of me, and I'm so ready to have him inside me, fucking me.

Bastian positions himself at my entrance, holding my gaze in the mirror. Slowly, he pushes inside me. I gasp as he stretches me in all the right places. He caresses my spine as he gives me a moment to adjust to his girth. It feels good, like he's scratching an itch I didn't know was bothering me.

Looking up at him in the mirror, my husband drips in sex appeal. Bastian is shirtless, his ab muscles contracting and tightening as he thrusts.

He grabs my hair and tugs it toward him, causing me to arch my back. Bastian leans in, placing his mouth at my right ear, and says, "Do you like watching when I fuck you?"

His free hand roams up and down my spine as he holds me to him. Moving his hand to my right thigh, he pulls it open wider, exposing his rigid dick inside me, pulsing, throbbing. We are connected, and I don't know where he ends, and I begin.

Panting, all I can moan out is, "Yes," as he bends me back over and slaps my ass again and again. It stings but feels so good as he massages out the pain between spanks.

"This is mine. You. Are. Mine." Bastian repeats every time he pushes his thick cock inside me.

I'm close to another orgasm. My pussy clenches, clamping down on his dick. Bastian fucks me harder, faster. He lets go of my hair and grabs my hips with both hands. His blue eyes are connected to my green ones. His neck muscles strain, and I know he's close to climax.

"I love you, Ana," Bastian grunts between thrusts. Reaching around my waist, Bastian circles my clit with his fingers.

I explode. My release sends me overboard in endorphins, rocking back and forth on Bastian's cock as pulse after pulse of my skyrocketing climax consumes me. He doesn't last much longer, coming right after me. Grunting as his seed is released, he moves slower in and out as the walls of my pussy milk all it can from his cock. Greedy bitch.

Bastian presses kisses on the back of my shoulder and smiles at me in the mirror. "That was something, huh?" he says as he pulls out, leaving his seed to leak out of my lower lips.

"Yes, it was," I agree as I move to turn on the shower. "Come, take a shower with me."

Bastian follows me into the stall. Before we get inside, I turn around and kiss him passionately.

"What was that for?" Bastian asks.

Shrugging, I grab his hand and pull him into the shower. I glance back at our reflection, and a shimmer along my neck catches my eye. I drop Bastian's hand to turn around completely to look at myself in the mirror. Immediately, I notice I'm wearing the emerald and pearl pendant again. What the fuck? When did I put this on? How is it that I didn't see the necklace until right now? This is crazy.

I really need to ask Bastian if he gave me this necklace or if I bought it somewhere. I touch the pendant, and immediately, I feel a weird connection. The stones feel alive. Whispers of nostalgia tingle my senses.

Bastian interrupts my thinking, tugging at my hair, and asking, "Hey babe, you coming?"

Forgetting what I was thinking about, I shove all thoughts to the side. Then I join Bastian in the shower, where he wraps me up in his arms and peppers kisses all over my face. Internally smiling, I decide it's time to stop any crazy thinking and start living my life.

Bastian claims me one more time in the shower before we leave for work that day. As I walk out the door, all I can think It's time I put together the missing pieces of my memory and move forward with my husband. Leaving dreams to sleep.

———

Later that day, I'm processing new orders before Janet arrives at *Morning Glory Arrangements*. We have had an increase in orders after the successful wedding last week. My little flower shop was featured in the local magazine, so now, business is booming. I'm happy about this, but I'm so exhausted that I don't think I can handle too much more work right now. Ever since I left the house this morning, I've been developing a painful headache.

Picking up a tall, crushed glass red vase I place it on the counter in front of me where I am working. Vitreous, lime green luster peaks through the broken shards of scarlet and ruby, accented by glimpses of fiery sapphire. I grab a bunch of sunflowers and cut off the stems so that both the height of the vase and the flowers are showcased. Bringing the sunflowers to my nose, I take a deep inhale, allowing their perfume to permeate my senses.

Suddenly, I am assaulted by a memory from a dream. The taste of exquisite sunshine tingles my taste buds, sending a shiver of desire throughout my entire body. The flavors are a roasted blend of nuttiness, salty, and a unique caramel that only this flower possesses. I look at the big blooms as a vision surfaces, *Jace...*, his face is but an echo, bouncing endless back and forth in my thoughts.

The doorbell jingles, signaling my favorite employee has arrived for the afternoon shift.

"Hi, Ana! How are you today?" Janet inquires when she sees me standing on the other side of the counter.

"I'm doing okay. And you?" I look up while talking, seeing that Janet already stands beside me. She moves fast, or maybe this headache's slowing me down.

"I'm awesome," Janet singsongs. "I had this amazing night with Adrian. Girl, I can't stop thinking about it." She fans her flushed face, pink from just thinking about whatever she did last night with her man.

I cast a knowing grin as I reply, "That's nice. I'm glad you and Adrian had fun." I add air quotes around fun. Winking at Janet, I tell her, "In fact, I'm changing my answer. It was better than okay. I had a great morning. It was fun too."

"Ooooooh…We both got it. That's nice." Janet adds, "But you look tired. Did that man let you sleep at all?"

Sighing, I respond, "He did. I slept plenty. It's not that."

I don't know if I should tell Janet about my dreams. What would she think if I told her I always think about a man from my dreams? And worst of all is that the man is not my husband.

I'm still debating whether to tell her when she asks, "Then what is it? What's making you tired? Are you sick? Are you pregnant? Do I need to take you to the doctor? Do you need some pain medicine?" She looks concerned, and I can't take it anymore. I break down.

Finally noticing the large boxes of fresh strawberries and mints Janet sat on the counter, I take a deep breath attempting to keep the sting of tears at bay. But the combined scents of the fruit and herb send a sob wrecking its way through my soul. As I begin, I look into Janet's dark brown eyes, "I have been having these weird, extremely vivid dreams. They are so lucid, so exhausting."

Janet looks confused. "So let me get this clear… Are you saying that your dreams are making you tired? Are you having nightmares? You know you had bad nightmares after the accident. If they're coming back, you need to tell Bastian. You need to make an appointment with your doctor."

Shaking my head back and forth, I stop Janet from continuing her rant.

"No. Not nightmares. Well, not always. It's just… I don't even know how to explain it. But for the past few weeks, every time I go to sleep, I have these dreams that feel… well, they feel so real at times. I think it's messing with my mind." I touch my head and rub my forehead. Just thinking about Jace and the Fae world makes it hurt.

"Okay, so every night you have the same dream?"

"Well, not exactly. It usually starts off similar, but then different things happen."

"Can you tell me what you dreamed about?" Janet inquires.

"Whew… it's strange. Please don't think I'm crazy, but in my dream, I'm in another world. A magical world similar to ours, but one that has Fae."

"Really, like in the movies or books? Like fairies?" Janet leans over the counter. "What happens in this Faery world? Do you have powers? Do you have pointy ears? What about wings? Please tell me you have wings."

She's asking so many questions all at once. The headache begins to throb at my temples.

"Janet, it's kind of like the movies but so much more beautiful. In my dream, I'm an Earth Fae who can control all Earth elements. I also have a little bit of water magic. It's magnificent, and at the moment, when I'm there, I love it."

"So what's the problem? It sounds like a nice dream," Janet states.

"The problem…" I sigh. "The problem is that in the dream world… I have a mate. A very attractive mate that is extremely sexy and knows how to get me worked up. In the dream, he tells me that we have been fated since we were children. Then when I wake up, I can't stop thinking about him."

Janet laughs. "For real? You are having dreams of another man, and that's what has you worried? Girl, I dream about Chris Hemsworth all the time, and that doesn't bother me at all. On the contrary, whenever I have a sexy dream, I wake up so horny that I roll over and fuck Adrian. "

"Wait, are you saying that it's okay for me to have sexy dreams about a man I've never met?" I ask, trying to see the silver lining to my messed-up mind.

"Of course. That's why they're called dreams, silly. They aren't real, even if they are wet dreams. It's just your body's way of telling you that you need to ride Bastian more often." Janet smirks as she giggles.

I listen to what she's saying, but I just don't know. If the dreams aren't real, then why do I feel so alive in them? This cannot be right. Right? My thoughts are becoming erratic, and I can feel my heart start to speed up.

Hurriedly, I admit my suspicions to Janet, "Janet, I just don't know. In these dreams, everything is so lucid. I can feel, smell, taste, hear, and see so much more. My senses are heightened. The experiences are so vivid that I'm getting my realities confused. What if…" I pause, cautious that what I'm about to say can bite me in the ass before continuing in a whisper, "What if this is a dream? What if now, us, right here is the actual dream world? Could I be waking in my real world to only fall asleep and dream about this place?" *And if so, why…* I leave the last part out. My headache pounds harder as I try to wrap my brain around what I just said. "I mean, Janet… Are dreams real, or is this just a figment of my imagination?"

"Well… I really don't know what to say about that, Ana. But I think you just need to relax." Janet comes near me and tries to calm me down. I'm getting frustrated because now that I think about it and said my thoughts out loud, I realize that I sound like a crazy person. What the fuck is wrong with me? Taking a shuddering deep breath, I close my eyes and try to just let it go. I need to stop thinking about this and focus on my shop, and Bastian, and getting past the trauma in my head.

I look at Janet and say, "I think you're right. I just need to finish work, get home, chill out. Order some food, drink a glass of wine, take a long soak in my bubble bath, and relax while I wait for Bastian to return."

"YES! That's exactly what you need. Then you can have some sexy time with your handsome man, too. Here, until then, I made you some tea. Sorry I was out of peach so you get the rose hip this time."

I laugh it out. She's so right. I look around my shop and

see that everything is organized. I take a sip of the tea Janet prepare, its sour yet fruit. The citrus flavor dances on my tastebuds. Already, I feel better, and my headache's disappearing. All that is left for the day is to finish making this one last order. Then I can go home and relax.

Later, after Janet and I finish packing the orders for her to deliver in the next couple of days, I leave to go home and do exactly what I said I would do. I need a break from my dreams. I need to go to sleep and just NOT dream at all. I don't think I can keep this up. I can't keep dreaming about Jace. It pains me to think like this, but I need to move on. He's not real. It's just a very good dream. I need to wake up to my real reality.

CHAPTER
Twelve

THREE DAYS HAVE PASSED, and I'm feeling much more relaxed. I haven't had any more dreams, nor have I had any constant migraines. In fact, I don't even think about the dreams, which is helping me a lot. I can focus on the here and now. I don't worry about my confusing realities.

Every day has been a rinse and repeat of the same.

I wake up early every morning and cuddle with Bastian. We kiss, talk, and enjoy ourselves before we get ready together.

Usually, I make breakfast because Bastian takes his precious time getting ready. I really don't understand why he takes so long in the bathroom. I just do my business, take a shower, and get dressed. I don't wear makeup, and my hair is usually left down, drying in a mass of waves.

I never make things complicated for myself in the mornings. There's no point since I work with flowers and dirt. Most days, I just opt for jeans, a cute T-shirt, and sneakers. Then I leave Bastian to do his business, and he takes twice as long. I guess being that handsome takes a lot of work. I'm pretty sure the man has more hair gel products and after-shave balm than I have in makeup and hair curlers. He'll stand in front of the mirror for hours (okay, more like several long minutes) placing each perfect strand of hair in its place before he meticulously irons his starched shirts that I just picked up from the dry cleaners, again. The man's OCD and mannerisms are beyond me some days.

Once breakfast is ready, Bastian joins me in the kitchen, and we eat together.

When it is time to go to work, we kiss, then go our separate ways.

The workload is the same every day. People order flower arrangements for weddings, anniversaries, quinceañeros, funerals, and more. I love it; I love the busy. The more work I have, the less time there is to think about Jace and the Fae world.

I haven't dreamed at all, and I feel more rested… but at the same time, I want to see Jace.

Every time I look at myself in the mirror, I stare at the pendant and see Jace's dark eyes gazing into my soul. I haven't removed the necklace, and I keep meaning to ask Bastian about it, but then I forget.

Yet every time Bastian touches me lately, I have a moment of panic because I feel like I'm doing something really wrong. I feel like I'm cheating on Jace with Bastian, or maybe I'm cheating on Bastian with Jace. I don't understand these feelings, yet I can't seem to stop them.

Okay, so not thinking about the dreams hasn't been working out as well as I want. Something always makes me think of Jace. I can't seem to stop, and if I'm being honest with myself, I really don't want to stop thinking about Jace and those dreams we had together.

I know I love my husband, and I know I like the life we have together… but I wonder, do I need more excitement? Is that why my dreams have become so carnal, so visceral?

Those dreams felt very real and exhilarating. To think that I can have powers is beyond amazing. I want to go back to the dreams and feel that Earth energy that surrounded me every time I was in the forest with Jace. I miss the feeling of the magic, but more, I miss the smell of him, the musky, salty woods that I know so well.

I want to feel free, to be one with the forest, one with my powers.

But those things are not real, and I can't seem to control when I have my dreams. Three days since the last one. Three dreamless, restful nights that leave me wanting more.

But every time I start to really think about Jace, I notice my head feels funky. It's like something prevents me from thinking about that other reality. If I can even call it that.

If I think too much about it, the pain intensifies. It leaves me with this horrible headache and heart-wrenching sadness.

So I work a lot and stay as busy as possible. I barely have the time to think about Jace or anything besides the job.

Besides, Janet is always talking nonstop, which also helps me not to think about Jace. I appreciate the distraction, and her non ending tea supply

Today, for example, Janet has not shut up about her family drama. Apparently, her family does not like Adrian. Janet is mad at her brothers because every time they see Adrian, they end up acting like assholes and get into a fight. It infuriates Janet because her brothers are still mad that she broke up with their best friend and teammate Thomas back in college. Whatever the reason for her detachment from Thomas, she always said it was necessary. That she couldn't afford to give him her heart for he was destined to shatter her to pieces. Once she mentioned something about him wanting to share her and she couldn't get past the idea of Thomas wanting anyone besides her.

However, Adrian doesn't care that he's not liked by her brothers, and he only has eyes for Janet. He thinks that with time, they will see his true intentions and see he's in love with their little sister, and nothing will stop them from being together. Even their delusions of unrequited love for their fellow brethren.

I agree with Adrian. Janet should let it go and focus on their relationship. That's what I'm explaining to Janet when she says, "I know you are right, Ana, but it makes me so mad that they act like assholes all the time. I don't tell them who they should date. I don't comment when they come around with yet another girl hanging off them. So why should they tell me who I can or cannot be with?" She's frustrated, pacing back and forth in the shop.

"I agree with that, but you know"—I shrug—"that's what big brothers do. They protect their little sister."

She huffs and looks at me. "I know they love me, but they need to stop. I really, really love Adrian, and I don't want him to leave me because of them."

I roll my eyes. "I think you're being a little dramatic, Janet. I know for a fact that Adrian is obsessed with you. Like borderline crazy. He won't let your brothers get in the way of your relationship, so stop making a big deal about this," I say to her while I'm working on a flower arrangement. I am actually surprised he hasn't attempted a proposal yet.

"Okay, I'll stop." She sighs and immediately perks up. "So… have you had any more dreams about your Fae mate?" she asks, wriggling her eyebrows.

She's so ridiculous. While I love her for it, I really don't want to talk about Jace. Yet Janet is relentless, so if I don't answer, she'll keep pestering me.

"No, I haven't dreamed at all these past three nights," I tell her.

"Really? That's a bummer. I wanted to know more about this dream man of yours," she says with a sad face. Even Janet is pouting. That makes me laugh.

"Well… trust me, this is a good thing."

"Why?" Janet asks.

"I don't want you to judge me, Janet, so please don't," I say while I look at her very seriously.

"Girl, you know that I would never do that to you. Come on, Ana, tell me. I really want to know. Why is it good that you aren't dreaming?"

How do I say this without sounding like a total bitch or a whore? Because that's how I'm starting to feel when I think about Jace and the dream world. A bitch because I want to demand that I go back, and a whore because obviously, I should only be thinking about Bastian, not some dream dude I concocted.

"It's good because I feel rested and wake up with energy for the day. I'm actually sleeping the entire night."

"But…" Janet says while she waves her hand like "come on, keep going bitch, I need to know more."

"But I really miss Jace. I know this sounds strange, like how can you miss a dream, but I do. I miss his kisses and his touch. And before you say anything, I know I have my husband. I know I have Bastian. But I can't seem to stop thinking that I have a real connection with this other man. Besides, he's sooooooo hot, Janet. Like aphrodisiac hot. I can close my eyes now and imagine his hard chest, filled with tattoos of the ocean. I can see those onyx black eyes; I can feel hair so soft and dark. He's strong and beautiful. Muscles that go on for days, I can't seem to stop touching them when I'm near him." I say all this with my eyes closed. Just thinking about Jace makes my heart race. I can feel the start of a headache forming.

"Dammit, girl," Janet replies, fanning her face as if she's overheated. "That sounds hot. Too bad it is only a dream because I feel you. After a wet dream like that, I'd want it on repeat, too. You know what you should probably do? You should use this to your advantage. Go home and fuck your husband's brains out."

I laugh. Of course, that's what Janet would suggest. "You know something? Maybe I'll do just that."

———

Later at home, I'm wrapping up cooking dinner when Bastian arrives.

He enters the door and cheerily says, "Honey, I'm home!"

I laugh at his silliness. "Hi baby, how are you?" I ask him. He looks so handsome today. Bastian has his dress shirt rolled up his forearms, and I can see the veins protruding from his tanned skin. I find muscular arms extremely sexy. But he also looks tired. His tie is loose, and his hair is disheveled like he raked his hand through it too many times.

"I'm tired, babe. We had a lot of patients today at the clinic. On top of patients, I had back-to-back meetings with the clinic board. But I do know one thing. I'm very happy to be home with you." Bastian takes in a deep breath before pulling me into his arms for a big hug. "Ana, what is that delicious smell?"

"That amazingness you smell is dinner. I baked a chicken, mashed up some garlic potatoes, and roasted broccolini."

Bastian smiles and squeezes me harder. I wrap my arms around him and notice he has something in his right hand. "What's this?" I try to look around and see, but he spins me away.

That's when he takes his right hand out from behind his back and presents me with a bouquet of white lilies. Looking at the flowers, I tilt my head in a bit of confusion. I really don't understand why he always gives me white flowers. Doesn't he know that I like colors? Trying to hide my puzzled look, I gaze up at Bastian and smile. "They are lovely, Bastian."

"Yes, they are, but you know what...? You are more beautiful."

"Aw, you are so cute when you give compliments. I don't feel pretty today but thanks." I give him a peck on the lips. "Sit down, and I will bring the food to the table. Do you want a glass of wine?"

Bastian makes his way to the table, and when I bring the food, he pulls me onto his lap, grabs my face with both hands, and says, "You are always beautiful. Every moment I see you, you take my breath away. I don't like when you say things like that. Okay?" He leans down and kisses me deeply.

I can feel the love that Bastian has for me. I sigh and answer back, "Okay, it's just that I have been at work all day. I'm pretty sure even with a shower, I'll still smell like flowers and dirt, and well, gross… I don't think I look nice right now. But if you think I am, well, I guess I am."

"Baby, you are perfect. Even if you rolled around all day in hay, I would think you're gorgeous." Bastian presses another kiss to my lips before he releases me. "Now, you sit. I'll pour us a glass of wine, and we can enjoy this delicious dinner you created."

Bastian and I finish our dinner. Afterward, he convinces me to join him in the shower. Bastian thoroughly cleans me up, washing and conditioning my hair, rubbing soap into my back as he lightly kisses my neck. The original plan was for me to seduce Bastian, but after our shower, he carries me to bed. In bed, he proceed to give me a foot massage that feels so good that I begin to drift off. The last thing I remember before falling asleep is Bastian humming and telling me that every-thing would be okay soon. "Soon, my love, I will make our dreams come true. I just need a little bit more time."

I can feel my body relaxing into a slumber. I snuggle closer into the warmth, nestling peacefully. My heart is content. Closing my eyes, I succumb to sleep, wondering if I will have any dreams tonight.

CHAPTER
Thirteen

I'M FADING in and out of consciousness. I can hear people around me, whispering to each other.

"This is the *fourth day* she has been like this," emphasizes a familiar voice.

"Son, if this is true, why are you just now summoning us today?" Another voice—deeper, rich, thunderous, masculine —holds a hint of concern.

The coolness of a rag wipes across my forehead. "Jace, she's burning up. You should have reached out the moment you realized something was wrong." Another voice, this one feminine, delicate, like a morning sea breeze. Her tone carries a worry that makes me afraid. But I cannot open my eyes or move my lips to tell her.

"I know, Mom. I know. I just thought… after the wedding and then finding her running through the swamp. I don't know what I was thinking to be honest. I just wanted to get her somewhere safe. I honestly thought the mating haze took over too soon, so she activated our backup plan, get to the cabin as fast as possible, no matter what."

Backup plan? What are they talking about? I wonder why we even needed a backup plan. Everything was laid out perfectly. We were getting married on the eve of the full moon in order to avoid my mating haze starting too early. Was that why we had multiple plans, because we were afraid that I was already going into heat?

"So you brought her home. You did right by getting her here. I'm glad you kept us and her parents informed, but you should have told us she was feverish and not acting normal much sooner."

"Father, I know." The voice sounds exhausted and frustrated. "Now, instead of telling me what I should have done, can we focus on what we can do now? What's wrong with Livi? Why is my mate so sick?"

Cool fingers caress my cheek before warm lips kiss my forehead. "Why did I come home to find you out front in our front yard, my love?" He's asking me, but I cannot reply. "Mom, she was soaked to the bone and passed out. What do you think? Could it be a symptom with the mating haze? Or maybe something happened when we forged our powers? What if Liv is pregnant already, and something is wrong with our baby?"

I can hear the panic in his voice. I want to reach out and tell him that it will be okay, but I can't move. My body feels too heavy, too tired.

"Oh, honey, shhh now. Calm down, my son." The female voice is trying to provide the comfort that I cannot. "Oliviana needs you to be strong and patient. I don't know what's going wrong either, but I do know our girl is strong. If she's carrying your child, use your water magic and look deep down. I could always find and feel you and your younger siblings when I was pregnant."

"Your mom is right, even I could detect your essence before the doctor could find a heartbeat by just checking the water."

"I tried a few days ago, but I don't even know what to look for. How would I know what to find?"

The other man interrupts Jace. "Look for the glow, son, then follow it, and you will know."

Look for a glow? What glow? Hmm... I start to think and mentally wander. How hard can it be to find this glow? His words spark curiosity in me.

"Okay, I'll try..."

"Good son, that's all you can do..."

Tuning out the voices as they continue to chatter, I focus internally. Glow, what does he mean glow? Is there a glow? How bright is the glow? Is there a color associated with this glowing? These questions parade in circles through my head

I don't have much energy left, but I continue searching, looking deeper inside. *Oh little glow, are you here? Where are you my glow?* I call out in my mind.

There. In the far recesses of my being, is a faint radiance blossoming from the surrounding darkness. But oh, it is most definitely a glow. I float closer and reach out with my mind, straining to touch the glow. As if understanding my intentions, the tiny radiant orb rises from where it is nested in the dark. Moving closer, I watch the glow bounce, hop, and buzz with increasing energy. I'm mesmerized by the animation of the glow. A giggle escapes me as the glowing orb whips around me, tickling and playing. So childlike is this glow. It reminds me of the butterflies that flutter through the forest. Flittering, touching, sensing this world as it explores the area around me before finally landing.

Realization sinks in as I finally understand what I'm seeing. The glow. This glow! Life. Jace and I made life. A feeling of blissful serenity washes over me as I take in our child, our own unique glow growing from the combination of our spirits, essences, and love. Barely existing, yet with so much potential, so much power.

Metaphorically in my mind, I hold out my hands, wanting to capture and hold the glow. The orb moves, vibrating intensely in my palms. For a moment, I worry that something is wrong. But then I'm left astonished as the glow emits an explosion of light, and the singular orb in my hands splits from one to two. Two perfect little identical glows.

As the light begins to fade, so does my remaining energy and consciousness. Before I drift back into a deep slumber, my last thoughts are the significance and importance of the two glows.

CHAPTER
Fourteen

STRETCHING, I try to shift my body into a more comfortable position. Glancing over at the clock, I see it's 4:55 a.m. Ugh, I'm awake before my alarm. I hate when I do this. I take a moment to steady myself for the day.

Rolling over, I go to cuddle up to Bastian, but the bed is cold. He's gone and has apparently been gone for a while. Maybe he's cooking breakfast like he did the other week. Deciding to go ahead and get my day started, I climb out of bed, turn off my alarm, and head downstairs to see if Bastian is in the kitchen.

However, Bastian is not there when I arrive. The only evidence that he was home at all is a lukewarm cup of coffee and a handwritten note. Popping the coffee in the microwave, I pick up the letter that he left on white cardstock.

My dearest Ana,

I hate to leave you so soon when I just got back. But I was accepted at the last minute as a keynote speaker for the national psychology

conference. The flight was before sunrise, so I didn't wake you up. Please don't be mad, but you were resting so peacefully. I know you haven't been sleeping well, so I couldn't bring myself to disturb you. Hope you enjoy the coffee. I'm sorry that it will probably be cold by the time you read this. Have a great day off. Enjoy your therapy session. I'll be home in five days.
Love you, -B.

Oh, well that explains the cold bed. I completely forgot that it was my day off again. The shop is open seven days a week, but I try to take at least one day every week to myself. I know Janet is more than capable of running everything for twenty-four hours.

Should I go back to sleep to get another hour or so of rest? I never really sleep in, so that seems pointless. Especially now that I remember my ten o'clock therapy appointment with one of Bastian's associates, Dr. Baron. It's our first meeting in person, and I'm nervous. We had a Zoom meeting from my flower shop the other afternoon to determine when I could come into his office for a face-to-face visit. He also inquired about the concerns I wanted to address when we met. So far, he seems nice enough, but I'm getting anxious now that it's appointment day.

So sleeping is definitely out of the question.

Instead, I choose to start my day. First, I make myself a quick breakfast. Then I grab my workout bag and catch an UBER to the local YMCA. A little physical exertion is always a good thing. At the gym, I go for a run on my favorite treadmill. Something about getting sweaty always helps me release stress.

After I finish my run, I head to the locker rooms. Smelling the hints of chlorine that permeate the air, I realize how nice it would be to go for a swim. It's still early enough and not a lot of people are at the gym, so I have the pool to myself. I change into a pale lilac-gray one-piece swimsuit.

Checking myself out in the mirror, I notice this suit is not very appealing. It hides my curves and makes me look bland, but it's the only one I have with me. I didn't bring the sexy white one Bastian likes. When did I wear it last? I can't remember.

The pendant still hangs around my neck, the dark-emerald, black, and copper colors clashing with the washed-out pigment of my swimsuit. Putting my questionable fashion choices to the side, I grab my towel and head to the pool.

During my fourth lap around the pool, I decide to take a break from swimming and practice diving. Climbing up to the top of the diving platform, I look down ten meters at the light reflecting off the water. A glimmer catches my eyes, and for a moment, I'm not staring at the pool, but instead, I'm on top of a cliff, looking down at a deep, dark blue pit. Shaking my head, I clear my vision, and I can see the bottom of the pool, including the robotic pool vacuum cleaner moving around, picking up leaf debris that has sunk.

Positioning myself at the edge, I balance and prepare for a tucked-forward flip dive. Launching myself upward, I rotate and turn, my body angling toward the water, my hands pressed together in a prayer over my head. I slice through the water with barely a splash.

At the bottom of the pool, I pause. Opening my eyes under the water, I have a fuzzy memory of diving from a cliff into a deep pool on the river. I can almost see shadows from tall kelp plants dancing off the surface and sunfish hiding underneath submerged tree trunks.

Following the bubbles that descended down with me upward, I rise and swim to the edge of the pool. Shutting my eyes, I try hard to remember the fuzzy memory. It takes me a couple of moments, but I gasp as the memory assaults my senses.

I can see everything clearly. I can hear, feel, and smell my surroundings as a vision takes over my awareness.

———

It was a sunny day at the river with Jace. It was our last afternoon together before he was sent off to the naval military training academy in the morning.

We were so young. I think I was about fifteen years old. Jace dared me to jump from the tallest ledge. The river pool was so clear that I could see the rocks and plants at the bottom. I was wearing a bright-green two-piece bathing suit, and Jace wore dark blue trunks. He looked so handsome. Even at the age of seventeen, he was covered in muscles.

I was so scared to jump because I've always been afraid of heights and deep water.

Jace kept reassuring me, saying he was there and he would catch me and never let anything bad happen. I was smiling at his beautiful words and could feel his adoration. So I jumped and squealed as the air rushed past, and I crashed into the water with a giant splash. Jace was soaked from his perch on the shoreline, laughing as I dragged my water-logged and aching body from the water. I couldn't help but return his grin; that was exhilarating.

———

When I open my eyes again, I'm smiling. That felt like a real memory. I can still hear the sounds of the river, the birds, and

Jace's voice. The smells of the surrounding forest taunt my nostrils before I inhale an obnoxious breath of chlorine.

This is so confusing. Why would I have a memory from the Fae world if that world is a dream? Did I dream this some other time, and now I remember that dream? Is this some sort of déjà vu? Or have I been dreaming about Jace my whole life and just now remembered them? Is Jace in all of my dreams? Having all these questions makes my head spin, confusing me more each time that I think about it. I need to get out of the pool. I need answers, and I won't find them swimming around here.

———

I quickly shower, get dressed, and walk over to Bastian's office building. Luckily, the Y is downtown and close to the medical district. I feel extra nervous as I walk through the doors since Bastian is not here and has gone to a conference. I don't know why I feel uncomfortable. It's not like I'm here to see Bast anyway, but something makes me uneasy.

I walk up to the reception desk, where a beautiful woman with rich caramel skin and tight blond curls types away on a keyboard. She's so focused on whatever she's working on that she doesn't see me when I come to stand in front of her.

I clear my throat, trying to catch her attention. I would go ahead and sign in, but there's no pen, and I'm not exactly sure where Dr. Baron's office is located.

When the receptionist finally looks up and sees me, she pauses her work, staring at me wide-eyed for a moment before realizing I'm trying to check in. A hint of shock flashes in her light, pale blue and peridot irises before she gathers her composure. Standing, the receptionist hands me a chart.

Wow, she's very pretty and so tall, I wonder if she's wearing stilettos or if she's naturally tall in stature. I mean, from my vantage point, she must be almost six feet tall. She's perfectly wispy with a whimsical grace as she greats me.

"Oh, Mrs. Murphy. What a pleasure to see you. Dr. Murphy mentioned you would be here today. My apologies that I didn't see you when you first arrived. I'm working on my newest manuscript and…"

"It's okay, perfectly fine, Miss…"

"Miss Vesper Aerie." Vesper reaches her hand out, welcoming me and shaking my hand with a firm grip. "It's such a pleasure to meet you, Mrs. Murphy. Bastian, I mean Dr. Murphy, always speaks very highly of you."

"Miss Vesper, it's a pleasure to meet you, too." It doesn't escape my attention that she called my husband by his first name before correcting herself. However, I let it go. I don't have time to dwell on that when I have my own issues to discuss.

Smiling, Vesper directs me toward a chair. "Mrs. Murphy, please take a moment to fill out this chart. One of our nurses will be out here shortly to escort you back to Dr. Baron's office in just a few minutes. Dr. Murphy already filed your insurance information and provided his Amex for any co-pays or other charges."

I reply my thanks to her and work on the paperwork while I wait. When I'm about halfway done, I a nurse hear my name called from a side door.

I follow the nurse through the door, and she guides me to Dr. Baron's office.

Dr. Baron's office door looks like any other drab, generic door. However, when the nurse opens the door and walks me into the room, it's as if I have stepped into another dimension. It's as if I'm in a living jungle even though I'm pretty sure the plants are all fake.

Everywhere along the walls are vines, ivy, creeping fig, and wild jasmine. In the far corners from his door, tree branches sprout out of the ceiling. I can almost imagine fruit hanging... maybe peaches.

Someone coughs loudly.

The world shifts, and all the greenery is gone from the room. Stark, barren white walls lay before me. I shake my head, trying to focus on the dark furniture that sticks out against the plain background

What. The. Fuck?

I try to consider what just happened when I hear another cough, closer.

Cough. He clears his throat. "Mrs. Murphy, I presume? I'm Dr. Baron, Bastian's associate. It is a pleasure to finally meet you in person." A large palm crosses in front of my vision, breaking my attention from the walls.

Dr. Baron offers me his hand to shake. It takes me a moment to come to my senses when I finally put my palm in his. I take a moment to look up at the exceptionally tall doctor. Bastian is over six feet, close to a foot taller than me at six feet and four inches, but Dr. Baron must be closer to seven feet in height. I'm about to ask him about his changing walls when he speaks first.

"I understand from our last Zoom conversation that you're struggling with sleep?"

"Uh.. yes. Hi. Um... Dr. Baron, it is nice to meet you in person as well."

Before I can continue, he uses his hold on my palm to turn me toward his desk. Pressing his other hand on my lower back, he guides me to a chair at the front. The move makes me feel uncomfortable, but as soon as we are at the chair, he releases me to sit down. It's a deep, black velvet cushioned lounger that I immediately relax into.

Dr. Baron moves around to sit behind the desk. "Now, Mrs. Murphy, why don't you tell me about your sleeping issues."

"I'm stuck. I don't really know where to begin Dr. Baron."

"Well, let's start with last night. How did you sleep?"

I think back to last night. Bastian and I had enjoyed a nice dinner together followed by a relaxing shower. I really liked the foot massage.

"It started out quite wonderful to be honest. My husband and I had a delicious dinner followed by an even better evening. I was so tired, I easily fell asleep."

As I'm telling my story, I begin to faintly remember highlights from the dream. "But then, I don't know. I had a nightmare, or at least I thought it was a nightmare…" Something good had happened, but I can't remember. It's frustrating because I think it might be important for the story.

"Do you remember anything that happened in your dream?"

"Bits and pieces, but then they fade away…"

"That's normal. It's our brain's method to process the recent day as well as reset and prepare for the upcoming one. We're not programmed to remember every detail of our dreams."

"Yes, I understand that. But… sometimes, when I'm actually dreaming, it feels so real. Like it's the reality in which I belong, not this one. Even though I can't remember them, that feeling lingers."

Dr. Baron takes a moment to ponder my words before continuing with his own thoughts. "Some people call that lucid dreaming, and many others practice the art. There are studies where people have even learned how to control the elements of a dream. You know you're asleep and dreaming, therefore you have the power to manipulate what occurs in the dream."

"Yeah, but why? Why am I having lucid dreams now?" I ask.

"Typically, they're caused by certain triggers, Mrs. Murphy."

"Triggers?"

"Yes. Usually, these stimuli are stressors such as anxiety or illness. I understand from Bastian that you had an accident a few months ago."

"I did."

"How has your stress and anxiety been since?"

"Definitely increased… after the incident. Well, I'm still recovering from a mild form of retrograde amnesia. There are experiences and memories that I cannot recall."

"What about your everyday emotions? How do you feel when you're awake?"

"Frustrated mostly… I mean, I find happiness here and there, especially at work when I'm surrounded by flowers. My best friend works with me, so she gives me a sense of comfort and someone to just talk to. But then there are times when I get angry, and I don't know why. I try to be understanding, to have patience, but sometimes it's difficult."

"I need to ask, but, Mrs. Murphy, have you been drinking lately? Maybe imbibing more than normal? I'm not trying to upset you, but I'm concerned about your health, and as a physician, it is important that I ensure we check every avenue before we determine the cause of your symptoms."

I take a moment because I don't know how to answer that question, that was completely random. Instead of giving a yes or no, I look at Dr. Baron and just tell him tentatively, "I don't think so."

"Okay. Good. Now, let's focus back on your day-to-day emotions. What triggers you to be angry?"

I know the answer automatically, but this is Dr. Baron. I'm not sure if it is wise to mention that most of my negative thoughts center around Bastian when he's gone. I'm sure it has to do something with being afraid of abandonment, and I should probably discuss this with the doctor. I don't know if I'm ready to pursue those deeply ingrained issues just yet.

He must sense my hesitation because Dr. Baron reassures me, "It's okay, Mrs. Murphy, everything you tell me is confidential. You are safe to speak your mind within these walls. No one will hear not even Dr. Murphy."

"It's Bastian."

"Ah, I wondered as much."

"What do you mean?"

"Bastian is a highly talented doctor and very much in demand within the therapy network. I can imagine his recent travels have not set well with you. Especially as you continue to heal mentally, emotionally, and potentially even physically from the accident."

Wow, he just nailed it. I have been nodding in agreement the whole time. "I think you're right. I miss him, and when he has to travel, I feel lost."

"That's normal. You're recovering. Do you have any others to reach out for support when Bastian is not home? Someone to talk to?"

"Yeah, my best friend. I told you, she works with me at my flower shop. I can go to her about anything."

"That is very good, Mrs. Murphy. It's important to have that relationship."

"Okay. I get that, Dr. Baron. But what does this have to do with my dreams and being able to sleep peacefully?"

"You know, Mrs. Murphy, *Medical News Today* once defined dreams as the images and stories designed by our minds while sleeping. These fantasies can be crafted to be entertaining, fun, romantic, disturbing, and sometimes even bizarre. We may not always understand why our minds create dreams in this manner. Indeed, we typically dream three to six times per night, lasting between five and twenty minutes.

"Occasionally, dreams may have some health benefits, such as helping the brain process information gathered during the day or healing after a traumatic brain event. It sounds to me that your brain is still processing what happened and is representing this through your amygdala, a part of your brain responsible for emotions. Therefore, when you dream, it feels real because your brain creates a chemical that makes the illusion sensible.

"You interpret them as real because your brain receives random signals that may represent some of your unconscious wants and needs. Tell me, Mrs. Murphy, is there anything you desire that you are not receiving?"

At the mention of the word desire, my body flares to life with passion. Memories of dark eyes exploring mine trying to memorize every facet of pleasure he's creating between us as he moves above me.

I blush. The thought already faded.

"Dr. Baron, there are many things that I want and need. Right now, a good night's sleep is the first thing."

"Then let's start there. I'm not one to prescribe medication, especially after initial visits. So tonight I suggest you do something you enjoy that will help you relax. Take a moment to meditate and reflect. Don't be hard on yourself; give yourself some grace and forgiveness. You have been through a lot and have a lot more to go through. I'm guessing that with several contradictory feelings occurring during the day, your dreams are trying to help you consolidate and work out what's bothering you. Let your dreams guide you to discovering your psychological balance and equilibrium.

"Now, before you go, let's plan a time next week to meet. I think these sessions will be good for you. I'll be interested to see how your dreams have changed by then."

That was a quick appointment. But before I realize what's going on, Dr. Baron escorts me out the door, and I'm saying goodbye to the receptionist... What was her name?

Damn memory.

Oh yeah, Vesper. Something tells me I need to remember her.

CHAPTER
Fifteen

AFTER MY APPOINTMENT, I'm over today. It has been an emotional roller coaster thinking about my discussion with Dr. Baron. I get another UBER to drop me off near my home so I can make a quick stop by the grocery store. My fridge is empty, and I need food to cook this week for myself, even if Bastian is gone. When I get home with several bags full of groceries, I put everything away and realize that the time has flown because it's already late afternoon. Making myself a sandwich with some chips, I start picking up laundry as I eat. While I'm dividing the clothes by color, another memory, maybe the remnants of a dream, slip into focus. This one is easier to grab.

————

I'm up, walking naked around Jace's room while he's in bed, covered up to his waist. I'm complaining and fussing at him about how messy he keeps everything. At twenty-two, he talked me into staying with him one night at his parents' castle. We had just finished having a few rounds of great sex, and I'm searching for my panties. I'm too tender for him to touch me again tonight.

Looking around at the piles of clothes and junk, I swear, Jace Seaborn is the most cluttered, messiest Fae ever. A mix of clean and dirty clothing is everywhere, and shoes are thrown haphazardly around on the floor. Not to mention Jace's gizmos and artifacts are just taking up space. He's worse than a mermaid collecting forks and gadgets. Fishing nets hang from his ceiling, acting as stages for his various trophies. Rescue floats, broken parts of coral reefs, an old ship steering wheel... I'm sure if he could, Jace would even have a sand castle. Speaking of sand, I pick up my dress and shake out the gritty particles. Why is it that when you are near the beach, sand gets everywhere and stays there?

"Jace, when we get married, I hope you know I'm not going to become your housekeeper."

"Morning glory, come to bed. Forget about the mess. That's why we have a maid in this castle, and they know how to clean it. They can clean everything once we leave the room for the day. Besides, you don't need panties."

I look at him from the corner of the room and say, "Really, Jace? You do know that once we get married, we will be living in the cabin. We are not going to have any maids there." I avoid responding to his comment about my current panty situation.

"We will when we are king and queen."

"Yeah, but that is a long time from now. We will live by ourselves until we become sovereign, and I'm *not* going to complain about this all the time. You need to start learning how to clean after yourself," I say to him.

Suddenly he throws a pillow at my face. "Just come back to bed, my love. I promise I will do better tomorrow. Besides, if you get back over here and let me make you come at least two more times we can go check on the progress of the cabin. And I'll make you come at a few more times as we check out how well the construction is progressing."

I laugh, this Fae! Thinking he can tempt me with multiple orgasms and my dream mountain home, he must forget I want that and more! I grab the pillow before it falls to the floor and throw it back in his face. It explodes into a shower of feathers. Jace slings another pillow at me, but I'm able to dodge it. I grab the edge of the covers and rip them from the bed, exposing my mate in all his glory. I draw in a sharp breath when I see his erection, stiff and pointing straight at the ceiling. Taking advantage of my temporary paralysis, Jace grabs me by the waist, dragging me onto the bed. Sitting on my legs, Jace makes me his prisoner as he begins to tickle me. Feathers float down around us as he joins our bodies and shows me exactly why I didn't need to worry about my panties and why I absolutely love his planning abilities.

———

I smile at the memory. Shaking my head, I go back to the laundry. Unexpectedly, I find myself thinking about this memory and the one that I had at the pool. I can't for the life of me figure out why the fuck I'm so messed up in the head.

Sighing, I finish putting everything in the washing machine and move to the kitchen. Maybe I should write a book about this shit. I need to get it out of my brain.

I think back to my meeting with Dr. Baron. It really bothered me that he brought up drinking. I don't think I have a problem.

However, I really need some wine if I'm going to continue having these memories from dreams of an unknown life. I always thought he said that dreams were easily forgotten, but apparently not these ones. Or maybe it was the therapy forcing me to remember them, or perhaps I was just creating my own delusions out of thin air.

With my wine in one hand, I go to the living room to ensure everything is organized. Paying close attention to all the details in my house, I notice that everything looks distinctively bland. It's all white. There is no color anywhere except the occasional shades of gray and other washed-out hues. Everything is just plain generic shades of white, white, and more white, like a picture from a magazine advertising an all-white schematic for a new brand of paint primer. This space doesn't look lived in. How long have we been here? There are no other pictures besides the ones of our wedding day. But even the photos are basic, slightly blurred, black-and-white images that could be found in any dollar store picture frame.

I walk from room to room, sipping my wine, observing the same trend throughout the house. This home is so boring. I should bring some colorful flowers from the shop tomorrow. Maybe a few sunflowers or a *Dracaena trifasciata,* the air-cleansing snake plant, to help enhance the ambiance of our home. A simple change to some of the decorative pillows from bleach white to more colorful ones would help bring some cheer to the place. I could also change the bed covers, maybe a bright-green quilt covered with purple and yellow flowers. I'm so obsessed with flowers and shades of color that I don't understand how the fuck my house has so much white everywhere. What was I thinking when I decorated around here? Did I decorate? Maybe we moved here after the accident, and this is what happens when my brain is on the fritz and Bastian has to make the decisions. Sighing internally, it's the best explanation since the man loves the purity of plain, drab, basic, and white.

After cleaning, I take a few minutes to do some online shopping for the house. I add a few brightly colored pink and orange throws as well as a clover green rug with blue accents to my Amazon cart when I realize it's getting late. Looking at the time, I see it's after eight o'clock, and I haven't heard anything from Bastian all day. I try calling him, but he doesn't pick up the phone. So I send him a quick text.

> Me: Hey babe, hope you are having a great time at the conference. Text or call me back.

I wait for a response, but the message stays on *unread* status.

Deciding to add one more message, I type and send:

> Me: Also, therapy went great. Thank you for suggesting Dr. Baron. Love You.

I almost sign the text, Love, -O but stop myself. I think about adding Love, -A instead but don't and just press send.

Around nine thirty, I'm cuddled up on the couch, reading the newest rom-com from my favorite romance author. This book is hysterical, with friends on vacation playing pranks on each other as they help one of their tribe find true love in the form of the boy grown into sexy man who runs the resort with his father. I can totally see Janet and I doing similar tricks on each other, and we wouldn't even have to be on vacation. Just bored at the shop. I go to pour myself another glass of wine and realize I have finished the entire bottle of Chenin-Blanc.

Feeling slightly tipsy and getting pissed that I haven't heard back from Bastian, I finally decide to take a hot bath. Infusing it with lavender oils and bubbles, I lower my body into the heat. The water is nice, relaxing the tension from my muscles. The buzz from the wine combined with the warmth of the bath makes me feel sleepy…. And strangely needy.

I begin fantasizing about the dream memories I had earlier in the day. I wonder what it would be like if they were real. If Jace were real. What would life be like? Sometimes Bastian is so distant that I no longer know who he is. Besides the few times we have been intimate lately and the horrible adventure to the lake, what else is there? Where are our memories? Would I feel less alone if I were with someone like Jace (or maybe Jace if he were real)? Thinking about the Fae sends tingles down my spine. Even if it was a dream, when Jace looked at me I felt like I was the world, that I was his queen. Visions from the dream jump to the front of my mind as I imagine Jace in the tub with me. I trace my fingers down my sternum, gently caressing the skin between my breasts before I squeeze my right boob. Settling deeper in the water, I open my legs and use my other hand to spread my folds. Circling my already stimulated clit with my index finger, I imagine Jace's mouth there instead. How would it feel if he were to insert a finger as he licks and sucks? What if he was kneeling between my legs, worshiping my body. How would he use his water magic to enhance our pleasure? The visual is enough to push me over the edge, toppling into an orgasm as I vigorously rub my own sex, calling out Jace's name, trying to prolong this feeling, this moment of ecstasy and relief.

With a lot of effort, I finish washing up and pull myself out of the tub. Definitely don't want to drown. I wrap up in a towel, not bothering to put on pajamas. When I climb into bed still damp, my thoughts center around Jace and his power over me and my dreams as I fall asleep to the *delusion that maybe… just maybe my dreams could be real in my sleep.*

CHAPTER
Sixteen

WHAT THE FUCK *did I drink last night? And why did I do that? Maybe I do have a problem...*

I ask myself as I cringe. Everything hurts, moving hurts, my head hurts. I try to pry my eyes open, but they're stuck. As I jerk upward, a pained cry bursts from my lips. My entire body shouts at me to lie down and go back to sleep.

Hands, rough, warm hands wrap around my shoulders and pull me into a chest.

"Livi, hey my morning glory, I've got you," a soothing, familiar voice tells me. Hmm... I like this voice.

My eyelids are still stuck together, so I turn my body around and cling to him as if he were my own personal life raft. Inhaling deeply, I get a strong whiff of my favorite perfume. Woods after the rain, musky amber, a forgotten ocean. Gasping, I force my eyes open and look into the dark depths of my lifeline, my Jace.

"JACE!" I cry out, grabbing him tighter and squeezing him to me. A sob rips through me as I bury my face into his neck.

Jace holds me, stroking my back, kissing my head as

torrent after torrent of tears breaks free from my eyes. His shirt is soaked, but he keeps me close, speaking softly into my ear. "Shhh… it's okay, Livi. Everything is okay. I'm here, right here." Jace grabs my hand and places my palm over his heart. I can feel the beat, strong and steady.

"Breathe with me, Liv," he tells me. Focusing on his heart-beat and breathing, I attempt to match his rhythm, breathing in and out as he does. Slowly, I can feel myself calming down. My heart rate normalizes. The darkness dancing at the verge of my vision fades away. All that is left at this moment is us.

"Jace," I say again, this time with more passion instead of panic. Looking up into his eyes, I almost forget everything, all my worries, all my concerns. I'm lost to him. He's the black hole that has swallowed me whole, and I happily let him. Desire floods through me like an electric current. Before I can think or stop myself, I crush my lips into Jace's, pulling him into a bruising kiss. Jace returns my kiss with just as much fervor, tangling his hands in my hair as our tongues battle for control.

I can't let him go. I'm desperate to have him closer. Rotating my body, I move to straddle his lap. Grinding down, we both groan as I smash our bodies together. "Jace… Fuck, Jace, I need…" I'm begging, pleading, whimpering for him to ease this ache inside.

Jace understands, and without words, he seems to natu-rally know what to do. Pulling apart long enough to lift my shirt over my head, Jace leans forward and captures one of my nipples in his mouth. While he sucks, he uses his other hand to reach between us, sliding between my folds.

"Fuck, Livi, you are so wet," he says when he releases my breast before his mouth catches mine. I lick the bottom of his lip as he glides his tongue into my mouth. Pressing down-ward, I rub my sex along his length. But there's too much fabric in my way to get to what I want. Why does he have clothes on while I'm naked? I don't worry about that thought. I just push up enough to reach between us and free Jace's cock from his trousers to align us.

As I slowly sink back down, Jace maintains eye contact with me as the tip of his dick breaches my pussy. We both moan as he thrusts upward and fills me, stretching me to fit his girth. I begin riding him, matching the pulses of his cock moving in and out of me. Jace grips my ass in his hands, yanking me up and down at a punishing pace. I'm so close, I can feel the orgasm building deep within my being.

Without warning, Jace flips us, and I land on my back on the bed. Pushing back inside, he begins to fuck me fast and hard. It's exactly what I want, what I need. "Jace," I cry out again and again. My orgasm suddenly crashes over me when Jace swivels his hips. I'm done. Panting, moaning, I'm a quivering mess as Jace continues to pound into my pussy. He's relentless, and when my first orgasm ends, the second one begins, or maybe it never ended at all. My legs wrap around his waist, pulling him in deeper, his cock hitting my G-spot in all the right ways. His hand snakes down, fingers circling my clit. Another orgasm wrecks my body, causing me to spasm, clenching, holding Jace's throbbing erection on lockdown.

"Fuck, Livi," he pants as he finds his own release. Kissing my swollen and tender lips, Jace rocks his hips slowly, pushing his seed deep inside. The walls of my sex refuse to let him go.

Foreheads together, Jace looks into my eyes before he sighs, then gently slips out of me and pulls me up to sit. I don't like the storm brewing in the depths of his eyes.

"Jace, what's wrong?" I cup his cheek.

"Livi, I think I should be asking you that question. Do you remember anything from the past few days?"

"Umm... maybe... not really. Why do you ask?"

My confusion must be written all over my face because

Jace has a worried expression as he says, "Well... hmm. How do I start?"

"At the beginning, that's usually a good place," I tell him with a wink.

"Haha, Livs. Okay. Well then, do you want the good news or the not-so-good news?" Jace huffs out a breath of air he had been holding. "Hmm..." I ponder, bringing my fingers to my chin before I give my best "thinking man" pose. "How about we start with the not so good and work our way to better?" I suggest, leaning into his warmth.

Jace encircles me in his arms, rubbing his palms up and down my triceps. I know he's contemplating how to share what's bothering him. I give him a little nudge with my shoulder. "Come on, honey, it can't be that bad. Can it?"

Jace releases his grip around me, running his long fingers through his messy hair. "So... the other morning... I... fuck, Livi, this is harder than I thought it would be." The frustration is clear in his voice. "Okay. I'm going to just state this as simply as possible. Please don't read into it until we finish discussing. I just have to say it.

"So... four mornings ago, we had a tropical low move through the area. When I woke up, it was storming. I know I haven't shown you everything here at the cabin yet, but we have an auxiliary shelter where my horse, Obsidian, is kept. You were snoring and sleeping so well that I thought it would be safe to leave you while I ran outside to make sure the extra building was secure with all the wind and rain. You may not remember, but Obsidian can get grouchy when he feels ignored, so I wanted to spend a few minutes attending to his affections.

"When I returned to the cabin, I found you lying outside in the rain. Soaking wet in the mud and burning up with a fever. You kept begging me not to touch you, but I had to bring you inside."

Jace's entire body shudders. I hug him close and press a kiss to his chest before he continues.

"When we got inside, you were screaming and trying to escape. Yelling about an orange-eyed monster chasing you. I held you for hours. Rocking us back and forth until the nightmare finally passed.

"Livi, it was horrifying having to witness your fear and not knowing how to help. I mean, we have had a lot of adventures and many scrapes, cuts, and breaks, but nothing like this. You were so feverish, and I couldn't bring you back to me. I was so lost.

"After the first night, I reached out to my parents. Unfortunately, it took them two days to get here. During that time, I had to do something I'm not very proud of and I'm afraid you will hate me forever. I'm the worst mate." Jace drops his head into my neck, and I can feel the cool wetness of his tears. Jace never cries.

"What… what did you do, Jace?"

"Oh, Oliviana my love, I'm so sorry, but I had to put you into a temporary resting state until help arrived." Jace is shaking, his tears falling onto my bare chest. "It was the only way. You were so scared, and with the fever rising… I had to, and I will forever regret the decision because I didn't have your consent. You were never given a choice. My parents agreed it was the best decision and have gone home, waiting for my next plans."

"Oh, Jace. My love." I pepper kisses all over his face and wipe away his tears as I tell him, "It's okay. It really is okay. You protected me. You protected us." I move his hand from my waist to my stomach and press it down.

His eyes lock onto mine. I smile and say, "Now, why don't we move on to the good news."

Jace's lips are on mine before I can continue. This kiss is gentle, intimate, and filled with awe and excitement. I hold my hand over his as we both look down at my belly. "You know?"

"Yes, I know."

"Liv, we made a glow. We are having a baby."

Kissing Jace, I grin as I reply, "No, honey, we made two glows."

"No…what do you mean no…wait… Two? Two of what, my love?" He nuzzles my neck, grounding me back to reality.

"Glows. Jace. There are two glows."

Jace pushes me back, astonishment written all over his face. "Two, two glows? Are you sure?" Jace looks confused for about two seconds before recognition crosses his features.

"Yeah… at some point, I remember hearing voices and someone talking about a glow. So I decided to investigate. When I found our little glow, well, it split, and then there were two…"

"Glows! Two! Livi, what do you mean it split?"

"I saw them, Jace! It was so surreal when I found the glow."

"I thought you said two?"

"Hush. I'm not done yet. As I was saying, I found the glow and picked it up in my hands." Jace has a quizzical look across his brow. "I know, I literally held a metaphorical glow. But that's when the best part happened. As I was cradling our glow in my hands, it started to vibrate and shine brighter before it suddenly split. Then there were two. Two glows, Jace! Two glows! Do you know what that means?"

Understanding fills his eyes as he claims, "Two. Livi, yes! Twins, oh my beautiful morning glory! We are having two babies!"

Jace pulls me up from his lap to stand before he wraps me in a hug and spins me around the room. "Livi love. We made glows! We're going to be parents." He's smiling, and happiness radiates from my mate.

I'm giggling and crying. "Yes, my love. My mate. We did it. Everything we ever dreamed about is coming true."

Jace pounces, grabbing my face as he kisses me deeply. This time, his kiss burns and drips in intensity and adoration. Laying me back gently, he moves between my legs. "Livi—"

I don't let him continue as I grab the back of his head and pull his lips down to mine. Arousal builds inside me as I hold my mate. Now that we know I'm pregnant, the aching pangs of the mating haze are gone. In their stead, a new appetite builds. Eagerly, I wrap my legs around his ass, guiding him where I want him. I know we just finished having sex less than thirty minutes ago, but I need him. I need him now, and by the looks of his extremely hard cock, he shares the sentiment.

Surging forward, Jace fills me once again, and I draw my breath in sharply. It doesn't matter how many times this Fae claims me, the first entry always hurts in the most delicious way. Holding Jace to me, I'm mesmerized by how he loves me. This isn't fucking. This is so much more. This is lovemaking.

The cadence at which he undulates above me, his cock setting perfect time and harmony against my clit as he sinks in and out of me, has me moaning and begging for more. Each thrust brings me closer to the climax I'm desperately seeking. I can't get enough, never enough. Matching his rhythm, I try to increase the friction by moving my hips in time with his.

The smugness of his grin as he knowingly pushes me toward an orgasm is too much. The way he pivots his hips as he pinches my clit is too much. I spiral out of control. The power of the orgasm releases something from deep inside me. Earth and water magic mingle, connect, dance, explode.

Memory upon memory assaults my mind. Our first meeting with our mothers. Our first dancing lesson. When we snuck out of the castle for the first time, and then got caught for the first time sneaking out. Our first kiss. The very first time Jace made love to me on the forest floor at The Fabricate. His official proposal. The wedding. Our honeymoon and plans around my heat and the mating haze. Fuck! Everything floods back to me as Jace takes my body to new heights, flying me beyond the moon and to the stars.

CHAPTER
Seventeen

OLIVIANA'S MEMORIES

"OLIVIANA!" Jace calls from the surface. "Get your sexy ass back up here right now!"

He knows I can't hear him because his voice is too muffled under the water. Besides, I'm on a mission. It's his fault, and he knows it. It was his bright idea to go free diving at the reef. And now I've seen something that I want, and I'm determined to swim down there and get it.

"LIV!" the suppressed sound barely makes it to my ears. If he keeps distracting me, I won't have enough air and time to get to my target. I'm so close, two more feet to go, I can almost touch... suddenly, I'm jerked backward and pulled upward. My captor's tight grip is unyielding.

When we break the surface, I force my elbow back as hard and fast as I can, stabbing directly into ribs. The arms holding me release, and I turn around. "JACE, what the fuck! I was almost there! What were you thinking?"

Panting hard while treading the waves, Jace retorts, "Livi... I swear. If you don't get your ass on the boat right this instant, I'll drag you up there myself and then spank that ass until it's so red you won't be able to sit for a week."

"But Jace..."

"No buts, dammit, Liv. I was serious when I told you not to go down that far. It's not safe that deep, well, not for you yet." Jace swims over to me, pulling me to his body with one arm while keeping us floating with the other. Kissing salty kisses to my wet forehead, he continues. "In a few more years, I promise I won't worry about you and water."

"After our formal bonding, right? Then I'll have some of your water powers, so I won't be able to drown?"

"Yes, and I will have some of your Earth powers. Maybe sooner if we can figure out how to forge our magic together. But until then, no risks. I'm not taking any chances."

"Fine…" I pout. "But you have to go down there and find the shiny thing, or I'm diving back down when you're not looking."

"Okay, Livi." Jace laughs. "What did you see? I'll go down and retrieve it for you."

"I'm not sure exactly. But I saw something glimmer under that big shell near the yellowish staghorn coral."

Jace boosts me up onto his boat. "Okay, stay here. I'll be right back." He dives back down. The water is clear enough I can watch his descent. It doesn't take him long to find what caught my attention. Surfacing, Jace holds a rare black pearl in his palm.

———

The mud is thick in this area. I feel like I have been treading for years through the muck even though it has only been a few hours. Exploring caves has become a new obsession of mine. Every time Jace comes to visit, I drag him to another one in the region. The one where we are today was abandoned thousands of years ago. There are legends that it holds the greatest treasure known to Earth Fae—jewels, stones, and precious metals. However, the myth is that the cavern is also haunted. Yeah, by mud and more mud.

"Livi, how much farther before we can turn around?" Jace asks from behind me. I'm ahead of him with the firefly torch lighting our way while he carries my digging and climbing equipment. I know he's getting exasperated, but we're almost there. I can feel it.

Putting my hand in my front pocket, I finger the pearl in there. For the past year, I have carried Jace's black pearl everywhere. Ever since we started venturing into this cave, the pearl has started to warm and get hotter. It's not hot enough to burn, but the intensity changes depending on the direction I face. I proceed forward, focusing on the course where the pearl is the warmest. Eventually, we reach the end of a tunnel, and the pearl goes dormant.

"Now what, Livs? Where to next?"

"Hmm. I think we're here, Jace."

"Okay, so what are we going to do now? What's the plan, love?"

"Shh, Jace…" I quiet him. "I'm listening."

Pressing my ear to the rock wall, I release my Earth magic. Feeling, scouting for something… *Ah! There it is.*

"Jace! Hand me the pick, quick. I need to dig right here." I point at the area.

"Livi, just use your Earth powers to move the ground out of the way."

"Seriously, and risk bringing down the Earth around us? Plus, where is the fun in that! I want the sweat, the blood, and the fucking tears. Now give me my pick!"

Jace laughs at my antics as he pulls my digging tool from the backpack and hands it to me. Shaking his head, he mutters, "Only my morning glory refuses to use her gifted powers and wants to do things the hard way."

Holding the sharp end at the angle I need, I squint and aim for my target area. Then I begin to dig. Heaving my body into every strike, I keep working as the rock crumbles away. Sweat trickles down my spine, beading across my forehead. It takes me a few minutes, but slowly, I carve at the stone until I break through into a hidden chamber. No bigger than my shoe, inside the hole a green light radiates outward. I reach in and feel an object. Pulling it out, I look down and see that I'm holding a dark-green emerald.

———

We are at The Fabricate. For years, we played here as children, grew to know each other's bodies as young adults, never truly realizing the significance of this place in our lives.

I'm holding the emerald in my hands while Jace holds the black pearl in his. Our wrists have been woven together with a soft copper cord. Delicate, iridescent fabric has been draped around our shoulders, binding us intimately together.

Today, we will use The Fabricate's anvil to forge our stones and powers together. Today, I turn twenty-four. And today, a few weeks to our formal wedding, we will finally be bonded. The wedding is just an event for our friends and family to party. Today is the day we finally start our lives as bonded mates, true mate bonded.

After years of research, Jace and I finally figured out how to forge the two stones we found on our adventures together. The new jewelry that we create from this combination will act as a conduit for our magic to merge. Finally, we can share our powers. The excitement in me builds.

Jace whispers words in an old language. His voice calls to the blacksmith and nymph, requesting their ancient power to wield our hearts into one. Jace's chanting gets louder and picks up speed. I can feel my Earth powers tickling at the surface of my skin. I join Jace, harmonizing with his melody. Slowly, I can feel his Water powers envelop me, hugging me closely as my own magic spreads toward Jace, caressing him in Earth magic. Blue and green light radiates around our bodies, swirling together in an animated dance. At the same time, we hold out our hands, the stones resting outstretched in one palm while we join the others. Palm to palm, we watch the stones levitate and spiral around each other. The pearl and emerald spin faster and faster, then crash into each other. A loud thunderous crack is followed by a bright orange light coming from the stones.

Slowly, they float back down into our waiting hands. I close my hand around the object. I can feel our combined magic pulsing in it. Opening my palm, I look down and see a pendant forged together. The emerald sits on top of the black pearl nested in a copper cage. Looking over at Jace, he shows me the object in his palm. A matching, simple copper band with tiny pearls and emeralds alternating back and forth.

Jace smiles at me before taking the pendant, stringing it around a chain, and placing it around my neck. I slide the ring on the fourth finger of his right hand. I think about how his left hand will hold our formal wedding band in just a few weeks.

Staring back at my mate's deep, dark eyes, I can feel his heartbeat and sense his love. When I lean in toward him, Jace grabs my face and kisses me. The kiss begins slowly, but the passion increases as our powers reemerge and pulse around us, completing our mating bond.

———

"Oliviana! Oh, my goddesses, you are so beautiful! Your dress, it is so stunning! I can't believe you went with the green." My best friend and maid of honor, Milly, fawns over me as she helps secure a cathedral veil on my head.

My mom straps my feet into a pair of soft leather slippers. "Indeed, you are the most beautiful, my daughter."

I love my mom. She and I look very similar. Some say that I'm a replica of her. I've always loved that about us.

With her strawberry-blond hair, fair skin, green eyes, and

the same body shape that has curves in all the right places, we almost look like twins. Our only differences, I'm a little bit taller than her at five-seven, and she has a few grays in her hair.

"Thank you, Mom. Thanks, Milly. I'm so excited to marry Jace. I can't believe this day has finally arrived," I tell my mom and Milly. My eyes start to tear up from all of my emotions.

"Don't you dare start crying, Livs. I did a damn good job with your makeup, and you will mess it up if you cry," says Milly, trying to hold back her tears.

"I know. But I can't help it. I'm just... just so excited! I can't wait to start my life with Jace. Married, as Fae husband and wife." I sigh.

"Girl, you and Jace already have a life. This is just a formality. It's not like you're a virgin or anything."

Milly's comments make me blush. "Yes, Milly. I know. But still... we may have been fated mates our entire lives, but this is a big step to our future as a family. This is huge, and I'm scared. I don't know what to expect during my first mating heat."

Milly rolls her eyes. "You are silly, Liv. You both already have sex. It's just going to be more amped up."

I groan in frustration. Turning to my mom, I ask her, "How did you feel when you had your first mating heat?"

My mom smiles and answers, "Well, honestly, honey, I was aroused all the time. Everything that touched me, I felt very deeply. Sensations electrified my entire body. Unlike you and Jace, I had just met your father, so it was very confusing. I couldn't get enough of that Fae, yet I barely knew him. Even though he still took care of me and my body and more so once we found out we were pregnant with your older brother."

"Oh, okay. So I guess, it's not bad..." I say while Milly giggles. She's such a twat and acts like a teenager anytime we talk about sex. I'm also giggling because, for the life of me, I can't imagine my mom being aroused all the time. She's so poised and always in control of her emotions. Imagining her in that state is a little bit difficult.

"Don't laugh, you silly girls. I'm being honest with you. Trust me, once you have been in that state for thirty days, you will understand," my mom retorts. Then we are all laughing.

"But for real, Mom. Do you have any advice? I mean… thirty days. That's intense."

"Hmm… My best advice, Oliviana, is to stay hydrated and make sure snacks are available. Don't worry about timing or how long. Just have fun and enjoy your mating moon. If all goes accordingly, in about nine months from now, you'll be a very busy mommy and wish for this month of reprieve with your mate."

"Aw, Mom."

"Aw, Queen Mama," both Milly and I say at the same time.

Turning around, I take a moment to really admire my wedding dress in the mirror. It is layer upon silken layer of dark-green tulle. A deep V plunges between my breasts, exposing the pendant Jace and I forged. The drop waist accentuates my hips. Long sleeves are embroidered with a prismatic rainbow of delicate lace flowers. The same patterns are hemmed into the body of the skirt. The train stretches behind me for at least five feet. Emeralds, sapphires, and black opals are embossed in a copper crown commissioned by my father that holds my veil in place.

I look over at my mom, and now she's wiping away her tears.

"Mom, don't cry. You will make me cry, and then we will be a mess, and Milly doesn't have time to fix our makeup."

"Yes, Queen Mama. I can't handle the tears right now. We can cry later in the ceremony," Milly says, coming to stand beside us. She makes grabby hands toward us so we can have a group hug. Milly has always been silly. We grew up together, and our parents are friends. My mom treats her like another child and knows we cannot deny the girl a hug.

I love my friendship with Milly. She's honest and knows how to have fun. We used to escape the castle to play outside with our powers. We always ran around and got ourselves in trouble, but we had fun. I wouldn't have made it through my teenage years without her. She's my person.

After we hug, Milly leaves the room, and my mom gives me another hug and kiss before saying, "I'm so proud of you, Oliviana. You have become an amazing young woman. You and Jace will have a great marriage. You won't have to worry about anything with him because he will give his life for you and your kids." I smile and say, "Thanks, Mom. I love you."

"I love you too, sweetheart." Mom turns to leave me alone in the room. "Alright, sweetheart, I'm going to tell your daddy to come on up and get you. Don't let him fuss with your hair, and for Fae's breath, please make sure he has his coat buttoned up."

A few minutes later, there is a knock on the door, and I'm so nervous. I know that it's probably my dad coming to collect me. I'm wondering how he will react to seeing me in my wedding dress. I'm his baby girl, and I'm leaving the castle where I grew up. I won't get to see him all the time. This is hard for me, so I can't imagine how he feels.

Walking toward the door, I open it. However, I see that it's not my dad but one of the new healers on the other side. I didn't even realize he was back from his medical studies. He smiles and nods, indicating he wants to enter the room. He's carrying a tray with a metal jug that has condensation on the outside and a small metal cup.

"My princess, your mom asked me to give you something for the nerves. Here, I have some medicine and water that will help you relax."

"Thank you so much. I really appreciate the thoughtfulness." I grab the smaller cup, and he serves me water from the jug. Tilting my head, I quickly swallow all the liquid before handing him back the cup.

Out of nowhere, I suddenly start to feel dizzy. I put my hands on my head because everything is spinning. Closing my eyes, I pull in a deep breath.

The healer reaches out, touches my arm, and asks me, "Are you feeling okay, princess?"

"No, I'm not feeling okay at all," I answer. The world around me is getting darker. Lights dance in my periphery. I sway and almost lose my balance. Moving to a chair, I collapse. "Something's very wrong. Everything is spinning…"

The healer moves close to where I'm sitting, watching me intently. I look at the cup in his hands, then back up to his face. He's just watching me, staring at me with bright-blue eyes.

"What's going on? What was in that medicine?" I manage to ask.

"Shh… Ana. It's going to be okay. Relax, don't fight it." The healer is still staring. He's standing over me now. I'm gazing back into the depths of his eyes. The blue spins, and flames of bright orange dance in his irises.

"Huh…" My head feels so heavy on my shoulders. My eyelids are drooping, and it's hard to keep them open. "What do you mean, don't fight it?" I yawn. It would be so easy to go to sleep right here, right now.

What am I supposed to be doing?

I feel the hand of the healer on my shoulder. I peer up at him, bright-blue eyes morph into orange, snake-like orbs that glare back at me. "What…. What did you do?" I ask breathlessly.

"You are mine. You will be coming with me."

I try to move and get out of the chair, but my body doesn't respond. I can't move anything. The healer bends over to pick me up. He throws me over his shoulder, my wedding gown trailing us as he leaves my room. I'm trying to move, to hit him in his back as he carries me away, but I'm paralyzed.

Tears are the only things escaping, leaving a wet path down his shirt. I try to cry out, to make noise, but the only sounds are whimpers.

"Ana. Calm down. I'm taking you home, where you belong."

I try to stay conscious, but as he begins to descend the stairs, leaving the comfort of my bridal chambers, the world goes dark.

———

The room is frozen and dark. When I wake up, I'm alone and shivering. I look around but cannot see very much. No moonlight filters through the windows. I can only see stars twinkling above the dark forest canopy. Feeling around, I realize I'm in a bed, wearing only the sage green slip from under my wedding dress. Laying at the edge of the bed is my wedding dress.

I can't remember how I got here. Where's Jace? Did we have so much fun at the after-party that he just tucked me into bed?

I get out of bed and feel around for a torch. I need some light in here.

Finding one close by on a table, I use my Earth magic to create enough friction for a small spark and bring the torch to life. It's so cold that I can now see my breath as I exhale.

Moving around the room, I see a door reflecting the light from my torch. I go to open it, but it's locked. I touch the door surface, which is cold, like solid ice. Pulling my power to my fingertips, I reach out to sense the composition of the door's materials. It's iron. Fuck. One of the few things my Earth magic cannot control.

Holy shit. What the fuck is going on? Why am I here? The last thing I remembered was Mom and Milly getting me ready, and then Daddy came up…

Wait. *My dad. He never made it. The HEALER! What did he do?* The medicine, the dizziness?

Why? Why would he do this?

I slam my palm on the door in frustration and lean my forehead against it. I need a plan. I need to escape and find Jace.

Looking back around the room, I start looking for another way out. The window is small and up high, but maybe I can get to it if I move the table underneath. I rearrange the furniture and climb up on the table. I can get to the window, and as I reach up, I realize I can push the bottom pane upward. I push the pane up as high as I can. Standing on my tiptoes, I pull myself up. The cold is coming in quickly through the opening. My fingers already ache from the low temperatures as I grip the edge and peer over. I must be about ten feet up. I can jump that. But it's cold, so cold.

I climb back down and rush over to the bed. I won't be able to tie it up perfectly, but at least my wedding dress has enough layers that it should protect me from the frigid weather. Throwing my dress over my slip, I grab the torch and return to the window.

Hoisting my body up, I wiggle through the small opening. My head points down, ass up, but I'm out. Angling my body to the side, I drag my legs out of the window and drop.

"OUCH!" Gravity hurts. I hit the snow-covered ground on my side. Standing up, I dust myself off and get a good look at my surroundings.

Cold, dark woods every which way that I turn.

In the distance, I hear the neighing and footsteps of a horse coming in my direction.

Panicking, I press my body close to the building so the rider doesn't see me.

Trying to sneak a peek, I move around to the corner and immediately come up against bright, snake-like orange eyes.

"AHHHHH!" I scream. I turn to run, but the creature grabs my arm.

"Ana! Stop!"

I turn back and slam my torch into his face. Then I take off running into the forest.

The leaves and sticks from the forest floor poke into my feet as I run. Briars pull at my hair and tug at my clothes as I push myself forward. The chill of the night seeps into my bones. Fog blankets the forest, so I can barely see my hand in front of my face.

Faster. I need to run faster. I'm already pushing myself to the limit, but I have to run. I have to get away.

My mind is a whirlwind; all I know is I have to keep moving, going faster and farther before I'm caught. I can't remember what's chasing me and why I'm running. I just know I cannot stop. I cannot let him catch me.

In the back of my mind, I wonder how I know it's him chasing me. But I do know it's him. *Who is he?* I ask to no one as I increase my speed.

But no matter how fast I go, I can hear him behind me. Several feet at first but now I can feel him at my heels, reaching out to grab me and pull me deeper into the forest.

A small whisper across my shoulder into my ear, "Livi..." causes me to turn my head around, and there he is. Giant onyx eyes, the color of the deepest ocean, peer right at me.

Shocked at the intensity of his gaze, I stumble over a root, causing me to tumble. I try to correct my balance by rotating my torso, but this only causes me to launch myself into a free fall. Slowly, I see the rock approaching as gravity brings my body to the forest floor. I already know that the fall will hurt long before my head hits the rock. Right before contact, I hear my name louder this time, as if he's screaming for me, "LIVI!" And then all the world goes dark.

CHAPTER
Eighteen

THE SUN RAYS warm my face, and I take a deep breath. Stretching out in my bed, I'm sore. My pussy aches, it throbs. I reach out, feeling for Jace. That was some epic sex last night. I'm so backward that I'm trying to recollect what day it is.

I keep my eyes closed as I roll over. Oh geez, I'm more than just sore; I'm nauseated. When I pry open my eyes, my stomach roils. I can feel everything moving. My alarm blares, and I reach across and slam my palm down on the button to shut it up. Sitting up, I notice that I'm covered with a white bedspread, white sheets, white room. *Damn, if a dream is that good that I'm still sore the next morning, I need those more often.*

Remnants of other world adventures dance in the back of my mind.

I can still feel the wetness pooling between my thighs.

How much did I drink last night? It was one thing, feeling myself up in the bathtub, but sheesh, how much did I ingest to be dreaming about all-night proclivities? I think back to the question Dr. Baron had asked about me and alcohol. Maybe he's right. Perhaps I have a drinking problem that's causing some of my dreaming issues. And maybe even emotional fluctuations.

I can't recall exactly, but the evidence of this hangover suggests I drank a lot. My stomach tightens and rumbles. Everything is about to come up.

I yank the cover away from me and stand quickly. Bad idea. I cringe and hold the bed.

"Well, that just made it worse," I say out loud to an empty room. I try to walk to the bathroom because I know that I will puke at any moment. But I feel so dizzy. I don't know if I will make it to the toilet in time.

By some miracle, I manage to make it to the porcelain throne, albeit stumbling and acquiring bruises as I go, and empty my stomach. I hate puking so much. Whenever I have a stomach bug, I do everything I can to prevent being on my knees worshiping the toilet.

What the fuck is wrong with me? Why do I feel so bad? I've had plenty of alcohol-filled nights, so why is this so much worse? I'm thinking about all my drinking regrets when I notice that I'm in my white bathroom in my home with Bastian. It's at this moment that I realize that I fell asleep last night after drinking a whole fucking bottle of wine. The entire thing! I have to remember to never, ever drink wine again, well at least not a bottle in one night.

After emptying my stomach, I flush the toilet and rest my head on the rim. Slowing, I take deep breaths, waiting for the world to stop spinning.

After about ten minutes, I start to feel better and decide I need a bath and to brush my teeth.

I take my time in the tub. I need to wash away this hangover.

While soaking, I think about what happened yesterday.

I was right here in this tub touching myself, thinking about Jace. Oh my goodness. Did I really come with his name on my lips?

Yep, I sure did. Am I supposed to feel bad about this?

I hesitate in my answer.

Nah, I think…It's like Janet says "Dreams are not real." That means that I can do whatever I want in them and all is going to be okay. *Flicking my bean to dream Jace isn't cheating on my husband*, I tell myself.

Maybe what I'm dreaming could be one of my past lives. What if that life ended tragically, and I didn't live a happy ever after so it's coming to haunt me?

That could be a possible explanation for why I'm having these vivid dreams. It can also explain how I can remember instances that happened when I was growing up.

Yeah, that's it. I keep trying to convince myself of this because the other explanation is that I'm fucking crazy.

I really don't wanna get out of the tub, but I have to. I still feel like shit.

My head pounds, and I have a bad taste in my mouth, making my stomach turn again. I don't think that I will be able to go to the shop today. Sighing, I get dressed in comfortable pajamas, then grab my phone to call Janet.

Opening the phone, I notice no texts or calls from Bastian. The texts that I sent him last night are marked as sent but not read.

What the fuck? Why is he never answering his phone?

Do I need to worry that he has another woman? Better yet, would I even care if he has another woman? Shaking my head, I call Janet.

"Hi, girly, what's up?" Janet answers.

"Hey, Janet, I'm calling because I'm not going to make it to the shop today."

"Why, what's wrong?" Janet sounds concerned.

"Well, I woke up feeling like shit and puking. I'm going to stay home and rest. I don't want to make you sick."

"For real? Does that mean that you are finally pregnant and that I'm going to be an aunt?" she asks with too much excitement for this early in the morning. She's fucking crazy, always talking about me being pregnant.

"No, woman, I drank a whole bottle of wine last night, and today I'm paying the price of that mistake. That's why I feel like shit. It has nothing to do with me being pregnant."

All of a sudden, I remember that last night, I dreamed that I was pregnant. Is it a coincidence? What if I'm pregnant? When was my last period? I'm counting the days since I had my last cycle and concentrating so hard that I don't hear Janet's response.

"Ana, are you there?"

"Yes, I'm sorry. I just got lost in my thoughts."

"I know what happened. You ARE thinking about being pregnant. Am I right?" She pesters me to admit she might be right.

How the fuck does she know what I'm thinking? Okay, she's my best friend, so maybe she knows me a little too well sometimes.

"No, bitch. I'm just feeling like shit, and I don't have the time to think about babies. Besides, Bastian and I haven't talked about that topic." Well, I really don't remember talking about it, at least not with Bastian. Another vague memory of Jace and I discussing baby names flits quickly across my mind, something using our initials, a J and an O.

"What? Ana, Bastian is crazy for you, and I know for a fact that before the accident, you guys were trying to have a baby. So if right now you are pregnant, well, he would be the happiest man alive."

Ugh… I hate when Bastian and Janet bring the fucking accident up in a conversation. It still irritates me that I have no recollection of said accident.

"Well, I'm not preggos, end of discussion. You will take care of the shop and call me if anything major happens. Okay?" I'm frustrated. I just want to go back to bed and rest.

"Okay, jeez girl, calm down. I'll take care of everything. Hope you feel better."

"Thanks. Bye." I hang up, not giving Janet time to reply. My frustration is changing to anger.

I still feel like shit, and on top of that, now I'm mad. I don't understand why talking about the "accident" angers me so much. I take a few deep breaths and decide to lie down and wait for my hangover to pass.

When I open my eyes again, it is very bright in my room. I turn and grab my phone to see the time. Shit, it's well past noon. Wow. I never sleep this much. But I feel so much better now. Standing from the bed, I brush my teeth again and try to eat something.

Opening the fridge, I see I have some leftover chicken and decide to make chicken soup with vegetables. I put on some music and start cooking. My stomach rumbles. I'm hungrier than I realized. I put some bread on the toaster and serve my soup in a bowl. When the bread is done, I grab my food and take a seat at the table.

This smells delicious. I grab a spoonful of soup and bring it to my mouth. Once the hot soup touches my tongue, I gag. My stomach flips and flops, and the urge to hurl is immediate. I run for the bathroom in the hallway and end up heaving in the toilet. I don't have anything on my stomach, but I still have the need to puke. *Where is all this gross coming from?*

Ohhhh whyyyy am I still feeling like this? I sigh when I'm done. Flushing the toilet, I walk to the counter to wash my mouth and face. I take a moment to analyze myself in the mirror. The pendant, I'm wearing the damn pendant again. I take a closer look, pulling the stones up to my face.

Bright flames flicker inside the emerald. A sudden light is emitted, penetrating my eyes beaming straight back into my brain.

Everything rushes back to me. *The dreams, they were my memories!*

I felt my babies. I felt their glow. I touch my belly and just feel for them.

Could it be possible? No, it can't be. But what if…?

Fuck, I'm so fucking confused. Why is this happening to me? What wrong have I done to deserve this?

My breathing becomes heavier, and my heart pounds. Jace, my mate, our babies, I can't stop thinking about the dreams. Fuckity, fuck, fuck. What's going on? Which world is real? What's reality?

I need to calm down. I need a plan. I need to go to the pharmacy and buy some pregnancy tests and see the results. If it's negative, I'm just going to stop thinking about Jace and the Fae world. This is getting out of control. I need to know. Once I know, I'll decide what to do.

But what if I'm pregnant? What would that mean? Bastian is the father, right? There's no way I'm pregnant by Jace since he's a dream, right?

I go to my room and get ready very fast. I throw on some jean shorts, a white shirt, and my flip-flops.

Once I'm at the pharmacy, I see so many choices for pregnancy tests. Standing in the aisle, I'm deciding which test to buy. There are so many, which one do I need? I decide to grab the one that says the results will either be the bolded word **pregnant** or **not pregnant**. I think that would make my life easier. I rush to pay and walk home as fast as I can.

I need to know now.

I get home, and I'm ready to take the test. Sitting on the toilet, I read the instructions on the label. *How hard can it be? Just pee on the stick and wait.*

But when I'm going to pee, nothing happens. Shit, I haven't had anything to drink today.

Pulling my pants up, I run to the kitchen and fill a cup with water and drink it. Thinking that I need a lot of water, I keep drinking until I'm full of water, and I can't stomach another drop. Now I just have to wait. And hope that the water doesn't come back up the wrong way.

After what feels like forever, but in reality, is like thirty minutes, I finally need to pee. "Yay," I say out loud.

Going to the bathroom, I sit on the toilet and pee on the stick. Placing the test on the counter, I wash my hands and wait. I sing the *Jeopardy* theme song in my head while I wait, then I sing it again because I'm scared to look.

I grab my pendant, and I feel relief. It's like this pendant gives me peace like it knows to soothe my soul. *What if… no….but what if my life as a Fae is real? What if this is a dream? What happens if I'm pregnant?* I'm contemplating all these things when the time is up.

Taking a deep breath, I close my eyes. I say outloud to myself, "Oliviana, you need to stop with this train of thought. They are making you act crazy. Just look at the test and see for yourself that you are not pregnant." Ignoring the fact that I just called myself Oliviana and Ana, I decide to do just that, I look down at the test.

Pregnant

My heartbeat whooshes in my ears as the stick flashes its final result.

Pregnant

I put my hand on my mouth and gasp. I look at myself in the mirror. My eyes are filling up with tears. *This can't be right.* I start to hyperventilate. My vision is getting cloudy, and my head feels fuzzy. I can feel my heart beating so fast. I press my hands to my chest. I can't control my breathing. This is just too much. I'm way too overwhelmed, too hot, and I tilt, losing my balance. Darkness surrounds me as I plummet to the floor.

CHAPTER
Nineteen

"JACE!!!!"

"JAAAAAAAAAAAAAAAAAAAAAAAAAACCCCCCC-
CEEE!" I scream at the top of my lungs.

Strong arms wrap around my waist, pulling me into a hard body.

I thrash, squirming to be released.

"LIVI! Stop! It's me, I'm here." Jace pins me down on the bed. He lays his body on top of mine, preventing me from moving.

"Jace, oh goddesses. Jace." I sob. Tears pour out of my eyes.

"Oh, Livi baby, what's going on, morning glory? I'm here, right here. Talk to me."

"Oh, Jace. It's the worst. The nightmares, they're real. I keep getting stuck. I don't understand why I keep going there."

"There? Where is there, Livi? What do you mean you keep getting stuck?" Jace questions as he sits up and pulls me onto his lap. He tugged his shirt off at some point, using it to wipe away my tears and snot. "Take your time, my love. What happened?"

"I don't know, not exactly. But Jace… every time I go to sleep, my dreams… They take me to this world where I'm someone else. It's not our world. It's plain and boring, but it feels so real." I tell Jace through sniffles. "I wake up and go to work. Come home and repeat. It feels as if I'm supposed to be there. It scares me how genuinely real it appears."

Jace traces soothing patterns up and down my arm while I shake in his embrace.

"Shhhhh… Livi, it's okay. You just said it. They're nightmares, dreams. It's not real. You're not there. You're here with me."

Jace pulls my fingers apart and places my palm against his chest. I can feel his heart beating. "This, Livi, this is where you are." Pressing kisses along my forehead, Jace pulls me in closer, hugging me to him as we rock back and forth.

Slowly, my breathing calms, and my tears begin to dry. I blow out a nose full of snot onto the shirt Jace gave me. Jace continues to hold me, silently loving me, comforting me as only he can.

"Jace," I start, unsure what I'm about to tell him.

"I know this sounds crazy, but hear me out, and then tell me your thoughts." I'm pleading with him with my eyes. I just need to get this out of my system. I know it sounds crazy, but I need to know if this is my reality. I feel like I belong here and not in the other world. In that world, nothing makes sense. I know Bastian is very nice, but I feel everything every time I look at Jace. With Bastian, I don't have that connection. With Bastian, what I feel is only sexual and nothing else. My life cannot be that one. Something is happening for me to be having these weird dreams.

"Okay, baby, talk to me," Jace answers me. He's looking at me expectantly, so I start from the beginning.

"So the night of our wedding, I was trapped in a cabin with an iron door. I escaped using the window, and when I was leaving the cabin, a man appeared on a horse. When I saw him from afar I got scared, yelled, and ran for my life. That's when you caught up with me and I fainted in the forest. You brought me here to this cabin. After that day, I have been having these weird dreams. Nothing is connecting. I remember getting ready with my mom and sister, waiting on my dad, getting trapped, escaping, and then you—"

"You mentioned these dreams before, but I didn't think they were a big deal. Livs, I need to know everything about them. Tell me all the details you remember." Jace interrupts me.

"Let me finish, please." I look at him and raise my hands so he knows I'm serious.

"In these dreams, I'm not here in Chrysoberyl with you. I'm in another world where everything is completely different. People dress differently, they wear clothes that are stiffer and have less colors. The people don't have powers and I don't think anyone shifts. But they have things like cell phones where you don't even talk, you can just use your fingers to send a message. They have moving carriages without horses, some of them they call Ubers and will take you wherever you need to go. And just like here, in my dream, I'm not actually alone. I'm married to a therapist who travels most of the time to medical conferences."

When I mention Bastian to Jace, I feel that he's tense. He's breathing hard and is fisting his hands on his sides. But he doesn't say anything and lets me continue talking.

"In this dream, I own *Morning Glory Arrangements*, a flower shop that stays so busy. I have a best friend there, too. Her name is Janet and she helps me out with the shop. She told me that I had an accident in one of the car things where I got hurt, and apparently, it has given me memory problems. That's why I can't remember when I got married to this other man or how I became a florist.

"Recently, I started remembering you and this world, and that messes with my head in the other world. I'm supposed to be happily married there, but I can't seem to stop thinking about you. I dream of you every time I go to sleep. Little by little, I've remembered our life here. I thought I was dreaming about my past life, but one night, I was so desperate that I drank a medicine that made me go to sleep. I wanted to come back to you. I needed to see you and be in your arms. But after I dreamed of you and was here… I ended up going back to the other world with the other man. Jace, I just don't understand, nothing makes sense."

"Okay, Livi, I know you're confused. I already told you that you have been sleeping too much. While sleeping a lot during the initial phase of creating our faeling is normal, I have been very worried about you and our babies. I need you here with me, awake, not sleeping. That world that is in your dreams is not real. I'm real. We are real," Jace says while grabbing my hands with his and placing them on his heart.

"Can you feel this?" Jace asks. I can feel a rush of energy that flows through our mating bond. It's a live string, a wire pulsing with our magic.

"I know you can feel this. This is so real, Livs. We have been together our entire lives and are starting a family. We will get married, and we will have these babies. But these dreams need to stop. Something is wrong here. I can feel it." Jace drops my hand and starts pacing the room.

"What are you thinking? What could be wrong?" I ask Jace. I need to know what he's thinking. Does he know what's happening?

"This doesn't make sense. Why are you having these dreams? Why are you sleeping so many hours? I asked my mom, and she told me to take you to the healer. I think we should do that."

Jace looks at me when he stops talking.

"But what if I fall asleep, and I'm no longer here? What if I go back to that world and can't come back?" I say to Jace, starting to tear up. I can't stand the thought of going back to the other world. I need to be here. But what if this is a dream? What if I'm confusing my realities? Can that be possible? I sigh. This is so exhausting.

"My morning glory, I will NOT lose you. If we have to ride to the castle at this hour, we will." He comes to me and sits beside me and grabs my face with both of his hands. Jace plants a soft kiss on my lips and looks at me. I can't stop the tears. They fall down my cheeks, and he grabs them with his lips.

"But what if this is a dream? What if the other world is the real one? I'm so confused?" I had to say it. The moment I say those words, Jace's face falls in devastation. He drops my face and walks away and looks really mad. I know my confusion hurts him, but I don't want to lie to him. I want to be honest. If there is a small chance that this is my reality, I need to know it. I can't keep living like this. I want to be happy, and I feel like this is where I'll find happiness. But how can I know for sure? Jace picks me up, hugging me to his chest. I try to remember more and fill in the blanks before the wedding. What happened to cause this delusion?

A black haze fills my head with an ache that steals my breath. I shudder through the gasp. The memory tugging at my mind disappears.

What were we discussing? Oh yeah, dreams. This is a nice dream, but I need it to stop so I can get back to reality.

Carefully, I'm placed back on my feet. I sway. How wonderful it would be to sleep right here on this comfortable... wooden? Floor. My mind doesn't put together what just happened in the past few minutes.

Looking up, I find dark onyx eyes looking down at me. I pull my brows together in confusion and frown. "I don't know... Jace. This is all. I mean, you are so sexy... But this is just a dream, right? I keep confusing myself. Ever since my accident... I know this is just a nice dream," I muse to myself.

I pat him on the chest, walking away to find a nice place to lie down.

I yawn. "You are such a se...xy... nice... dream..." I feel myself drifting off, slipping away, when suddenly, I'm backed up against the wall by a very angry, very feral male Fae. Blue flames rage across his onyx eyes as he captures my gaze.

I'm wide awake now.

CHAPTER

Twenty

JACE

THERE ARE moments in life that stop time in its tracks. Most of the time, these moments are defined as positive highlights in a person's experiences. Then there are the moments that devastate your entire being.

I'm a dream. Is that what she just said?

I don't even know how to reply to that statement. I can feel the anger brewing, ready to implode the world around me. *I'm a dream. She thinks that this life, this world, is a dream.*

Taking a really deep breath, I slowly open my eyes and look at my mate. I know she's nervous from the way she's biting her lower lip, and I move my hand to feel her pulse. Most days, I would be jealous of her teeth sinking into the soft, plump skin, but right now... I want to shake her. I'm so furious. I tighten my left fist on the wall beside her face, caging her against the wall. I move my right hand and rub my thumb up and down her neck. I want to offer her comfort, but the fury coursing through me burns.

I can see the tears forming and ready to fall in those emerald eyes that captivate my soul. Red rings line her eyes from previous tears. Her nose is even pinked and swollen from crying. Her breathing is ragged, and her heart races under my perusal. What I would give to just wrap my arms around her and hold my mate.

But…I'm afraid. I need a moment. And I need to know if she's serious.

"Livi…" I pause, count to ten, count to ten again, take a few breaths, and continue.

"My morning glory. This… What I'm about to say is difficult. For one, just putting it out there, but you're acting very strange right now. Irrational. I literally don't know what to do with you.

I'm listening to what you're saying and trying to be attentive and a good mate. But after everything, after all the years, the adventures… I'm at a loss…

"Honestly, Livs, I feel like you're gaslighting me. I don't know if it's the early hormonal signs of pregnancy or latent mating haze feelings… but me. A dream? Like what. The. Actual. Fuck. Oliviana."

I'm huffing. I gently move my hands from the wall, then turn away from her and step toward the kitchen. I know my face must be red. When I glance over my shoulder, I can see the fear in my mate's dark-green eyes. I can feel her confusion radiating through the mating bond. I know her words speak truth and honesty. But seriously, I'm over this shit.

I'm down to two options at the moment. One, take Livi to her parents and have her see the family healer. Maybe he can explain what's happening and whether it's a health issue. Or two, some motherfucker is about to pay for messing with me and my mate.

"Jace…" I hear the tentative whisper before I even look up at her. "I don't know how to explain… what to tell you…"

The pain at her thinking I'm just a dream causes me to give her the only reply I can.

"I know what you can tell me. Tell me that you are MINE. Tell me that you know this is real," I demand. Walking to where she quivers against the wall, I can no longer restrain myself. I grab her by the waist and lift her back against the wall, wrapping her legs around my waist. I press a palm to her chest, and I can feel her heart beating. The other delicately wraps around the back of her throat, sensing the blood flowing through her veins. I can hear the rush of water to her head as I press my ear into her esophagus. I'm sensing, feeling...

"But Jace..."

"No fucking buts, OLIVIANA!" I almost slam my fist into the wall. Instead, I get into her face. We are nose to nose, eye to eye. The small incisors that identify me as a Fae male peek past my gums. I can't help the tone as I try not to raise my voice at my mate. I want to scream, but I'm not the type for over broadcasting my voice just to be heard. I prefer logical, pragmatic approaches that are reasonable. Besides, my mother always told me a little honey goes a lot further than a whole bunch of salt and I have my prey just where I want her.

"You think I'm just a dream? What the fuck, Livi? You think this isn't real? You think that other place, that place you go when you are sleeping is real? I don't fucking get it, Livs. Are you fucking delusional? Does it feel like a dream when I'm inside you? When I'm fucking that pussy? When you scream my name, is it just a dream? Does it feel like that? A fucking dream that doesn't exist?"

Her eyes flash. A shadow crosses those emerald orbs. Her brows furrow.

My head is about to explode. I release Livi slowly, allowing her delicate body to slide against mine as I gently place her on the floor and walk away. I can't keep doing this. Dragging my hands through my hair, I move to the other side of the cabin. I want to break something. I have been patient and trusting that its just the mating haze, but I'm over seeing her hurt and confused.

I need her to confirm, to let me know she's mine, that she

knows she belongs here with me. I'm facing away from her when I finally hear her response.

"No," she softly replies, and my heart sinks. Her tiny hand reaches up to my shoulder, pulling me to face her but I refuse. "No, Jace. Listen to me. I said NO because it doesn't feel like a dream. Jace, this place, the memories, you… it all feels like coming home."

That's the only answer I need. My head snaps toward her, our gazes colliding. She. Is. Mine. The mating bond reverberates through my body. I rush to cover my mouth over hers, my tongue clashing with hers. When I back her into the wall this time, it's because I'm lifting her by the thighs and wrapping her legs around my waist so I can rub my hard-on between her folds as our tongues tangle and duel for control. My anger is dissipating, replaced by a primal need to prove my claim over my mate again and again, not because I'm angry, but because this woman, this Fae belongs to me. Like the fog fading away to the sun, just one statement from her lips and all the fury in me disappears. She's mine, and as I nip at her bottom lip, I decide that I will find out who is fucking with her mind. It has to be someone because that is the only explanation for Livi's indecisive condition.

"Jace…"

"Livi, I know."

"Jace… oh, Jace." She pants my name as I lavish open-mouthed kisses down her throat and across her collarbone.

"Say it, Liv. Tell me, tell me, Oliviana, that you know this is real. That we are real."

"Yes, Jace. This is real. This is our world. I'm home. You are my home."

I rip off her bottoms at the same time as I release my own length and thrust upward, filling her in one movement. If she thinks this is a dream, then I'm determined to show her the reality of what I can give her. I'll fuck her into believing this is real.

It's hurried, fast, hard. But I claim my mate. She moans my name as her fingers curl into my hair. But I'm relentless. I can feel her clenching around me. She tries to use my shoulders as leverage so she can top me from the bottom, but I know this woman, this Fae. She's my mate, and I have known the intricacies of her body long before she even understood the meaning of pleasure.

I begin to go shallow, only thrusting my head in and out. It drives her wild. She's convulsing, begging for more. I know she's close to an orgasm, but not yet. Not until she knows I'm her mate, that I'm her world, that I. Am. Hers. Reaching between us, I do her favorite maneuver and pinch the living daylights out of her clit before gently massaging it. It's all I need to set her off. The inner walls of her sex clamp down and clench. My balls tighten, and I can feel my own release building at the base of my spine. A few more thrusts and I'm a goner. My seed spills out, coating her as she milks me for everything. I'm spent.

Sweating, huffing, I lean my head into Livi's neck and kiss under her ear. She pulls my head back and stares at me.

"Jace. I know, I remember. I'm so, so, so sorry." She's crying, and I'm still fully sheathed inside her. This is not good. I need to fix this.

"Shh, Love. Shh." I kiss her tears away. "It's okay. We're going to fix this. Trust me, Liv. Can you trust me, trust our love? I know it's stronger than anything. We are fated mates, and nothing can stop that. No man or curse."

That's it! Livi's eyes open wide, and I can see her agreement.

"A curse," we both say softly at the same time. I look at her and repeat the words again. "A curse. Could that be what's happening to you, my love?" I ask Livi.

"That could be a possible explanation. But why would I be cursed? We are loved by our people. It doesn't make sense, Jace," Livi ponders. "If there is a curse, we need to figure it out now. I don't want to go back to that world. I just can't," she says to me. It breaks me to see her so upset. There has to be something we can do to make these dreams go away.

"I know, Livi. We will leave right now for the castle. Pack a bag and wash your face. I've got you, babe. We'll be okay," I say to Livi as I finally pull out and release her from my arms.

We start packing our bags, only taking the clothes and food we need to get to her parents' castle. It'll take us about three days to get there if we leave now.

CHAPTER

Twenty~One

OLIVIANA

AFTER THE REVELATIONS of both my intense sleeping bouts and the memory issues in the cabin, Jace and I agree we need to travel to my home so I can see the healer. We need to determine the causes of my afflictions quickly.

Every day that passes, the dreams are getting worse, becoming more nightmarish.

I wake up in the other world, completely alone. I get up, do a morning routine that never changes and wonder why my husband is never home.

Then, I go to *Morning Glory Arrangements*. I complete the daily bookwork and accounting, organize flower arrangements, send out deliveries, get ready for the next day's orders.

When I finish at the flower shop, I come back to the house, make dinner that I don't even remember eating and finally crawl in bed.

Every night I go to sleep, still alone in this mundane world.

During my last dream, however, I arrived at the shop and it was empty. Completely bare. I remember running down the aisles in between stainless steel benches, throwing open cooler doors, and finding nothing. No flowers, no vases, no clippers or trimmers. Just vacant space.

The only thing holding me together and maintaining my sanity is when I wake back up in Jace's arms as he carries me on the back of Obsidian.

The worry of getting better is exponential now that I have two more lives in my care. I don't want to keep going back and forth between realities.

The new second moon since our wedding is over. Nightly, the lunar waxing crescent grows larger in the eastern sky. Now that the days are warmer and longer, we decide to travel via Jace's horse to my parents' estate in the mountains. North of our cabin, it's a three to four day journey if the weather is good. Obsidian is a dapple gray horse that Jace has had since he was fifteen years old. Sid has a beautiful gray coat color with lighter hair that creates a pattern that looks like miniature galaxies on his body. He's majestic. Jace loves him because, for him, Obsidian is part of his family.

Luckily, the weather has been perfect. Myself, not so much…

It's been four long days sitting in front of Jace on Obsidian. I'm getting tired from the constant bouncing and sitting stagnant in the same spot. It was fun at first, rubbing my ass in Jace's crotch, but now… My back hurts, I'm cranky, hungry… my mind whispers, "And hangry, girlfriend," something Janet would say.

I shake my head. Janet, who is Janet? The dreams still haunt us. I go to sleep, absentmindedly musing that I own a flower shop, looking for a husband who doesn't exist. I wake up screaming, clinging to Jace for dear life every morning. And every time I wake up from another nightmare, he holds me close, strokes my hair, and speaks soothing words to me and the babies. He's everything I could have ever asked for in a mate. I hate that these dreams are happening to me. They have been the only factor slowing down our journey.

"Hey, stop that."

"Huh? Stop what, Jace?"

"I know that look. Stop it. This is not your fault. We'll figure it out. And if it takes longer than we want, so be it. We'll still fix everything. You are still my mate, and I'm still here, YOURS. And I will remind you of that fact every day and every night."

Yeah, Jace has to remind me every time I wake that this is the real world, that he's my foundation, my lifeline, my soul. I can feel it from my head to my toes that he's mine. But these dreams, they feel like they're getting worse. Like they're trying to suck me in and keep me stuck. I don't want to sleep, but with the babies already consuming so much of my energy, I can't help it. I can be talking to Jace, and suddenly, I just need a nap. I'm out cold before I realize I'm no longer awake.

Yeah, and then, no matter when I'm sleeping, it always ends in a nightmare.

"I'm trying," I tell him. "But it's hard. My head isn't right. I know that right now this is real, but when I start to slip… it's hard to climb back up that slide."

"I know, Livi. Soon, we'll be at your parents', and I know we'll find our answers there. Just hold on, my love. A few more hours and you will be soaking in your old tub while I rub your feet."

A memory… rubbing feet. I sigh. How nice that would be to pour a glass of wine and prop up my feet while my husband…

I startle awake. I can feel the drool dripping down my chin while also recognizing the trotting rhythm of Obsidian. Looking up, I see my mate peering ahead. A wet spot is centered right where I lay my head. Nuzzling my forehead into his chest, Jace leans down, peppering soft kisses into my hair as he lets me know, "We're here."

———

The doors to the castle burst open, and my mom comes running out. I'm in her arms before my feet hit the ground as Jace helps me dismount from our horse.

"Oliviana, Jace. You both finally made it." She's squeezing me tightly.

Reaching an arm out to Jace, she motions for him to join us. He wraps an arm around both of us, holding us together in a big group hug.

"Jace, Oliviana." I hear my father's booming voice coming from the entrance.

"Your Majesty, King Oryon." Jace offers his hand. My father gladly takes it and gives him a handshake before grabbing Jace into a hug of his own.

"Son, stop the formalities. You have been family for too long. Now, what brings you both to the castle so soon? Your mother and I figured we wouldn't see you two until after the next full moon."

"Daddy…"

"Oryon…" Jace and I both start to explain.

We pause and glance at each other. I nod, signaling for Jace to continue.

"We need to see the healer. Something's wrong with Livi… I mean, she's fine, but she's not."

"What do you mean there is something wrong with my baby?" my mother asks.

My mother is still holding me around the waist. She focuses on my belly, placing her hand on top of it. Her eyes grow wide as she whispers, "Oliviana."

I smile. "Yes, Mom. We got pregnant during our mating moon."

"You hear that, Oryon!" my mom exclaims enthusiastically. "We're going to be grandparents! There's nothing wrong with that. This is supposed to happen! I can't wait to spoil our grandchild."

"Grandchildren, Mom."

"Huh… children? As in plural? Not just one?"

"Yes. Jace and I are having twins!"

"Well, look at that. Good job, you two." My dad slaps Jace on the back. "Come inside, we have much to celebrate."

"Daddy, wait. Hang on. Jace is right. Yes, we are pregnant, but something else is wrong."

My dad looks at us quizzically before tilting his head toward the door and saying, "Well, let's get you both out of the cold, and we can discuss what's going on in my office."

We all follow my dad into the castle. Bypassing the foyer and welcoming room, we head straight for my father's personal office. More intimate than the throne room, the dimly lit space is filled with deep and comfortable leather sofas and recliners. Burnt sienna walls are adorned with paintings of our family as well as relics my father has collected during his explorations of the northern regions. A social table sits in the middle where you can stand or sit as you chat about news and ideas. My father's large and imposing cherry wood desk sits in the back of the room. A replica of the throne sits behind his desk. My father perches on the desk and motions for us to get comfortable on one of the couches.

"Okay, you two. Besides the really great news, what's going on? Jace, your father mentioned he came to see you at the cabin. But he didn't tell us that Oliviana wasn't well."

"Yes, sir. They stopped by last week. Livi was running a fever. We thought it was normal signs of early pregnancy. My mother advised us that this was normal."

Jace sits next to me, and my mother is on the other side. Stroking my hair, she's nodding in agreement. "Yes, I remember every time we conceived, I would burn with fever for days afterward. It always clears up and goes away to be replaced by the blush of pregnancy."

She presses the back of her hand against my forehead.

"You're not feverish now. But I don't see any blushing either. It's as if your aura is bleached. That's interesting."

"What? What's interesting, Mom?"

"Your aura has always been a psychedelic prismatic rainbow. In fact, I'm pretty sure the only color you don't like is white. The babies would only add to the spectrum, not cause a whiteout."

My mother looks at my father. "Oryon, call the healer. He needs to get here quickly."

"Okay, Lydia, I'll call for the Supreme Healer. It will take him a little while to get here from his chambers."

The doors to the office fly open. "OLIVIANA, YOU BITCH!"

"Janet?" I'm shaking my head. I can't believe this. Wait, that's not Janet...

It's Milly... My best friend, my maid of honor, my partner in all funny crimes. "Sooor… sorry.. I mean Milly. Milly!" I call out to her.

She's running into the room toward me. Launching herself into the air, she attacks, landing on me with a brutal squeeze. "LIVS! What the fuck? You come home and don't even let your best friend know!"

She looks over at my mate and slaps him on the shoulder. "And YOU! I expect that SHE would ignore me, but how dare you come home and not let me know. I'd figure you a better Fae than that, Jace."

"Milly, settle down. You're so ridiculous. They just got here. We barely have been in this room for five minutes," Mom says, patting Milly's head of wild red curls.

Milly rolls her eyes. "Queen Mama, I don't care. You are my other mother, so she's my other sister. And I haven't seen her in over a month since the wedding…"

"Yeah. About that." I start to say.

"Yeah, about that. What the fuck, Livs! One moment I'm fixing your veil, we are all sappy, and the next thing I know, your father is running out into the courtyard saying you're missing."

I start to say something, but she clamps her hand over my mouth.

"I'm not done." Milly scolds, "Then Jace over here finds you, sweeps you away to your little cabin in the middle of nowhere, and all I'm told is, 'Don't worry, Milly. It's all fine, Milly. She's safe, Milly. They are on their mating moon, Milly…'

"And you know what, I wasn't fine. I was stuck here, worried sick about you. Then I hear from the cook that my long-lost BFF has returned with her mate, and he can't wait to whip up a celebration dinner.

"AND NO ONE BOTHERED TO LET ME KNOW!"

Milly has collapsed into my arms, crying dramatically into my hair. She's hugging me to her chest, stroking my head. I pat her back and rub soothing circles up and down her spine. "Milly, I'm so sorry. It's been a weird month, and a lot has been going on."

Sitting up, she wipes her eyes. "But I missed you, and you promised we could talk every day."

"Milly… I promised I would talk when I could. I didn't say every day. Besides, I'm here now, so stop being extra and get off me."

Milly sighs theatrically. Jace pulls Milly off my lap, placing her where he was sitting. Then in alpha-mode Jace fashion, he pulls me up, takes my place, and resituates me on his lap.

Milly faces us and presses, "Fine. But at least tell me, am I an aunt yet?"

"Yes," I respond.

"EEEEKKKKK!" Milly screeches. "You are having a baby!" She's bouncing in her spot. Thank goodness Jace is absorbing all the shock of her excitement and not my ass.

"Two," Jace states.

Milly stops. Her eyes go wide before she screams again. "TWINSIESSSSSSSSSSS!"

Before Milly can continue her theatrics, my father interferes.

"Mildred Janet. ENOUGH," my father finally bellows. His patience with her silliness has come to an end.

Janet, Milly. A memory attempts to break into my consciousness. A wave of nausea rolls through me at the knowledge.

"Milly…" My pupils are blown out at my realization. "You… you were there, too."

"Livi, what are you talking about? Where was I, too?"

"In the dreams…" I grab her hands. "You were there. But you were not Milly… no, you went by your middle name, Janet."

"Girl, I obviously love you, but I haven't been in your dreams. I've been here in the castle. Alone might I remind you."

"I know, I know. But… Okay, let me start over. I need to explain what's been going on the past month."

"Besides lots of mating…" Milly starts, but I punch her in the side and give her a look that tells her to stop it.

Looking around at my parents, my bestie, and my mate, I take a deep breath before I begin. "So ever since the wedding night, I've been having these nightmares. Dreams that are so vivid, so lucid, I thought they were real…"

I continue telling my story, explaining what happens in the dreams. I tell them about being a florist and how Milly, well Janet, is my coworker. I describe my home and how it's white and boring. Finally, I bring up the fact that I have a husband in my dreams who is not Jace. I can tell my dad is getting angrier. I can't even look at Jace, but I feel him vibrating in rage.

I don't like reiterating what happened in the dream world, but I don't leave out any details… except the parts that contain sex... I just can't get my head around that just yet. Jace is the one person who has ever known my body, my mind, my heart, my soul. It doesn't make sense that I would ever dream about another claiming me as he does. I would never consent to anyone but Jace if I was in my right mind.

At one point during my story, Jace lifts me to the side and gets up, pacing around the room while I finish. Now that I'm done, we're all silent. I'm waiting for someone to speak, to say something, anything.

Finally, it's Milly who breaks the silence.

"Damn... girl. That's intense. So these dreams... you're saying that you thought they were the real world, and that this place, this world that is actually yours, is fake?"

"Yeah."

"Damn... that really fucking sucks."

"Tell me about it," Jace and I both say at the same time.

He pulls my torso to his chest, cradling me.

"King Oryon, Queen Lydia. I'm sure you can see why this is a big concern for us. It doesn't make sense that Livi's dreams are caused by the pregnancy or residual symptoms of the mating moon."

"Oliviana, do you remember what happened after Milly and I left you in the bridal suite?" my mom inquires.

"Mom... no, not really. Jace and I have gone over every moment from the time that you and Milly left, and Dad came to get me. But I don't remember anything except waking up in the cabin with..." I pause. More memories are knocking, begging me to remember them.

I shake my head. I can feel a migraine forming at my temples. I rub them while Jace rubs my back. Milly reaches over and rubs my shoulders. Tears leak out of my eyes. My lungs raggedly take in air. It feels like my chest is gripped in a vise.

"It's okay, Livs. We are all here, and you are home. We'll

figure it out. Don't worry about it, babe," Milly tells me, attempting to be reassuring.

Jace sits back down, readjusting us so I'm back on his lap. He wraps his arms around my waist while placing kisses along my forehead. "She's right, my love. We'll figure out what's going on. And if it is a curse, we can fix that, too."

"A curse…" Milly taps the side of her head with her fingers. A telling sign that she's either thinking of a solution or remembering some strange fact. "How would you have been cursed…? Better yet, I think you should definitely ask the Supreme Healer. He probably has a potion that can tell us if you've been cursed."

She looks over at my dad. "Well, where is he? Have you called Dr. Murphy yet? After all, he should know everything about Liv's health. He's been our own personal physician our entire lives, mine, Livi's, his own children…"

Visions of thoughts, the memoir of the older snake-shifter hybrid… Part Earth Fae, part reptile… A discussion about dreams… a moment celebrating the news about his son rising up to take over the family business. A feeling of pride for a lifelong friend… but they are gone within blinks of each other.

I try to continue thinking about the healer, but the back of my brain itches, and a burning sensation runs down my spine. An unknown anger breeds inside me the more I think about him. Something I forgot tries to emerge from the depths of my unconsciousness.

A knock sounds at the door.

"Come in," my father bellows.

The door opens slowly. We are all watching to see who is joining us. A tall dark figure walks in, pushing a tray of concoctions. My eyes go to him. Aged, bright-blue, familiar irises stare back at me.

I'm sitting on a couch. Explaining to my new therapist

about the crazy dreams that I started having after the accident...

"No... no, no, no, no..." I'm shaking, and I bury my head in Jace's neck. He holds me close.

Jace is trying to comfort me, asking, "What's going on Livi? It's just Dr. Baron, you know him. He's been your family physician your entire life. He delivered you, morning glory."

"No, Jace, no, it's not that. I don't know... maybe it is. My head... this is just not possible. I don't understand." I look over to the Supreme Healer. "I know I know you, Dr. Baron, but you see, just like Milly, you were in my dreams, too."

CHAPTER
Twenty~Two
SOME TIME LATER IN THE CASTLE MEDICAL CLINIC

AFTER LISTENING to me reiterate my dream story again to Dr. Baron, he convinced Jace to bring me down to his clinic for a proper examination. Now I'm lying on a bench, knees up, legs spread apart as he inserts a probe that should be able to see our babies and cast an image so we can see them, too.

Because they refuse to leave me in peace, my mother and Milly are also crowded into the exam room. We left my father in his office. He wanted to follow up with Jace's dad, King Jaxon, to inquire what he thinks about this situation. Then because he's just as extra as the ladies standing in the room too close to me, he's determined to have a celebration feast this evening to celebrate Jace's and my arrival. Sheesh! My family. I love them, but sometimes we just need to stay calm and figure out one thing before jumping to the finale.

"Queen Lydia, Mildred, it would be a lot easier to examine Princess Oliviana if you two would just wait outside in the lobby. I'm sure she would like to protect her decency and…"

"Decency bullshit, I've seen that girl's twat too many times. What? Our moms just threw us in the tub together as little girls. And besides, she came out of Queen Mama's vagina. So I don't understand what you are protecting my

Livs from and you can just maneuver around us. We're not going anywhere," Milly states pointedly. Stubborn bitch, she won't budge now. Poor Dr. Baron.

Dr. Baron continues his examination even though Milly proves her point and makes him maneuver around her and my mom. At least Jace is kind enough to stand at the other end of the little room. Or maybe he doesn't like seeing my girlie parts when he's not the one actively engaged with them. I can't blame him. I'm not enjoying the movements of Dr. Baron's exploration.

"Anything yet, Doctor?" I ask him.

"Almost, Your Highness, almost…" He's concentrating intently. "Ah, there they are. Alright, you four, are you ready?"

He doesn't give us a chance to respond before broadcasting an image of two dark little beans… two dark little beans that have distinctive little heartbeats. Two dark little beans that are our babies! Mine and Jace's. My heart is full. Tears are falling out of my eyes. Jace is by my side, wiping them away and kissing my face. Milly and Mom are also trying to squeeze in hugs and kisses wherever they can.

"Jace, Mom, Mills, you all, stop, please! I love you, but hang on one moment and let this Fae have a second." I'm giggling, overwhelmed, and filled with so much love and adoration I want to explode. My babies, they are really there.

"Doc, so if the babies are fine. What about the dreams? How do we stop the nightmares?" Jace asks.

Dr. Baron has removed the probe, cleaning up while Mom helps me do the same. "It's hard to say, Prince Jace."

"Yeah, but don't you have like a potion or something that can tell us if Livs is cursed?" Milly interrupts.

"Mildred… it doesn't work like that. Yes, there are potions, but I would have to compound them, and that could take some time, depending on the type of curse we're discussing. There are also certain venoms but those are terribly regulated and controlled."

Milly pouts. He just busted her bubble for an easy answer. I nudge her from my spot on the bed. "Hey, it's okay. There's always an answer, even if it's not right in front of our faces."

"I may have a solution, but I'll need to call in my apprentice. He just got back from medical school where he has been studying neuroscience and alchemy. Hold on while I summon my son."

His son? Which one… surely, he doesn't mean…

It hits me. Oh fuck. I know my husband from the dream world. I try to catch Dr. Baron, but he's already outside the room, calling out for…

"Bastian. Boy. Get over here. We need some of that fancy medical training I paid for."

Bastian.

Bastian Murphy.

Dr. Baron.

Dr. Baron Murphy

Fuck…

Bastian. Fucking. Murphy.

As if my thoughts called him into existence, he stands in the doorframe. His bright-blue eyes locked onto mine. They quickly flash to orange when he realizes that I know, and that I know that he knows I know.

"MOTHERFUCKER. BASTIAN, YOU BASTARD!"

I remember it all now. I remember Bastian Murphy alright.

I mean hell, he's been around our entire lives. Domineering and acting like a brooding older brother since we were all kids.

I remember him always hiding out in the corners, watching us kids play. He was a lot older when we were born but still very much a kid himself. I often worried if his brain operated on an entirely different level, maybe even the universe. He was so smart but socially awkward. He would never talk to me growing up until I was a teenager.

Yet he always cared for our bumps, scrapes, and bruises if we got hurt and his dad wasn't around. We used to joke that he must be a doctor fairy because he always had medicines, tinctures, herbs, and tapes ready to bandage all our injuries. It wasn't surprising that he followed in his father's footsteps and left to study medicine.

I haven't seen him ever since he came back from his medical training. Does he know what's going on? I didn't realize he had returned to being an apprentice under his dad… I didn't think they got along very well… but that's another story I don't have time to ponder right now.

Right now, I'm up and running at him before I realize what I'm doing.

I can feel the energy of my Earth powers vibrating inside me. Pulsing friction heats my insides. I'm about to… I don't know what. I just know I need to…

I don't get to finish my thought. Bastian has made it through the doorway and slammed the door shut. He's intently focused on me.

Under his breath, he's mumbling something.

"Oliviana?" Milly whispers.

"Fuck, Bast, what is the meaning of this?" Jace starts.

Bastian picks up a jar from a cart next to the door. He slings the liquid out in front of him. It arcs high before turning to dust and sprinkling down on everything in the room. He's quick, frantically moving his hands.

A spell. My brain recognizes what he's doing. He's about to cast a spell on everyone.

I'm still moving in his direction, but I stop when he throws his arms out to the side. Power fizzles from his palms. Electricity zips between his two hands. He slams his hands together, and the clap sends energy blasting through the room.

I hear a thud behind me. Turning around, I see my Milly has collapsed on the floor, a hand hanging on the edge of the chair she was sitting on. My mother looks stunned as she too begins to slump toward the ground next to me. As her eyes roll backward into her head, she sprawls out on the floor. Jace looks at me, reaching out to me with his hands. "Livi," he mouths to me as he, too, crumples to the ground. His eyes never close, just stare blankly back at me.

I turn around to Bastian. The room fades in and out. I'm feeling dizzy. "What… what have you done?"

I try to find something to hold and keep my balance, but there's only air. I stagger to the side and hit the wall. Bastian walks up to me. I slowly slide down the wall to the floor and stare up at him. "Why, Bastian, why?"

"Because, Ana, you are my dream, and we will have all of our dreams come true."

He bends over and throws me over his shoulder before walking out of the room. As he shuts the door behind him, I lift my head the best I can. I take one look back inside at my family, all those I love so much. They're not moving. The world is growing darker. I find Jace's eyes. The darkness in his gaze looking back at mine. I think about our babies. The world goes black.

CHAPTER
Twenty~Three

I BOLT UP.

My heart is racing. I touch my palms to my face to make sure I'm… I don't really know what I'm trying to do, or what I'm checking for, but I know I'm not okay. I pause. Bridging my hands across my nose, I take a deep breath.

"Steady," I whisper to myself. "Be steady."

I don't know what woke me up, but something is out of place. My body feels like I have been running a marathon or suddenly had to urge to join a kickboxing club with my girl-friend and had my ass handed to me by said friend. I had another nightmare I can't remember.

Battling my emotions, I take in my surroundings. I'm in my room. Early morning light shines through the windows. It's after six o'clock. I slept in… Am I off today or…? I shake my head and get ready to crawl out of bed when I finally realize I'm not alone.

SNORE…

Bastian lies next to me.

That's different. I usually wake up to a cold bed. I don't remember the last time I woke up to find him next to me.

On his belly, Bastian snores deeply, fast asleep. I look

down at myself, realizing I'm wearing a lacy camisole, all in white. I don't remember going to bed last night. When did Bastian come home? Did he put me in this? It would make the most sense.

I take a moment to watch my husband sleeping soundly. The copper streaks in his hair are more vivid in the morning light. I never noticed that before. He even has a widow's peak. I almost want to brush his hair back to get a better look because I don't remember that either. I thought he had a straight hairline and dark hair.

Bastian turns, curling into my side, wrapping an arm around my waist. At first, I think he's awake, but then he starts to snore again.

I analyze his face from this angle. His skin is fair. He needs to get outside more. We should probably talk about how much time he spends in the office or clinic and make some more outdoor plans. However, the memory of the last time we went on an outside excursion makes me furrow my brows. I sometimes wonder which of the two of us actually needs therapy.

The tips of his ears are not as pointed as I remember a vivid memory of my lips nibbling, teasing while…

Bastian snores again and rolls away from me. The momentary distraction forces me to lose my train of thought.

I'm thinking very hard to remember what happened the day before. The more I try to focus on the memories I want to remember, the more I feel the start of a migraine. Nausea is setting in.

I sigh and lie back down on my pillow. I'm looking at the white ceiling. Why can't I focus? What day is today? I feel all weird. Something is off, wrong. I pat my belly. Maybe I'm due for my period soon. It would explain these symptoms.

Forcing myself to get up, I move to the bathroom and do my morning routine. While peeing and contemplating the day ahead, Bastian enters that bathroom. He's way too cheerful as he walks over to the sink counter and asks me, "Good morning, beautiful baby. How did you sleep?"

He smiles at me, and I look back at him. Bastian looks tired. His eyes are sunken, and I can clearly see dark circles have formed under his eyes. Even the bright blue has dulled to a weak gray. I don't understand how he can sound so excited and look that exhausted.

"I slept okay. Another nightmare, but it's nothing I can't handle. How about you? You look really tired. Did you get any sleep?" I reply.

I'm concerned. I can't seem to remember what happened the previous days or even this past week. Everything is blank... And Bastian looks like walking death. Or are we coming down with something? After the last viral outbreak a few years ago, I've tried to make sure we have herbal remedies and medicines to keep us healthy. But that only goes so far in today's society.

I finish my business with the toilet and go over to the sink to wash my hands and start brushing my teeth. Looking at Bastian through the mirror, I can see him looking at me. It feels... weird. Like I'm his prey, and he's ready to play before he enjoys his meal. But instead of feeling sexy and aroused, I feel wary and nervous.

"I slept okay. I'm just so tired. With all the travel to these back-to-back conferences, I haven't had the time to rest properly," he grumbles, walking toward me. "Besides, nothing is more comfortable than sleeping in my bed wrapped around my beautiful wife."

I have the toothbrush in my mouth as he stands directly behind me. Bringing both his arms to circle my waist, Bastian leans in close, placing his head on my right shoulder.

"Then go back to bed. Sleep some more," I tell him. "I can wake you up later. I'm taking the day off today so I can even have breakfast done for you in a little bit. That way, once you are rested, you can eat. Maybe we can watch a movie or binge-watch that new Netflix series. We can do anything you want."

I bend to rinse my mouth.

Bastian moves my hair to the side and starts kissing the back of my neck. It feels nice to have him here with me, but something is off about this. I'm not getting the warm fuzzies. Instead, a chill sneaks down my spine.

He mistakes my shudder for arousal, not the sudden fear encompassing my body.

"I think I just need you, baby," Bastian claims while roaming his hands all over my body. His left hand goes up my belly and starts rubbing my left breast under the camisole I have on while his right hand moves my hair farther out of the way so he can kiss me on the side of my neck and behind my ear. I lean my head to the left so I can give him better access to my neck, and close my eyes. Bastian moves his right hand down and starts playing with my other breast. I'm trying to focus on the feeling of his hands on me but I have this nagging feeling that something is not right. I press myself back into his body, seeking warmth, but only find the hard wall of his chest.

Bastian's caresses are rough. I moan from the pain and try to get him to stop, but he claims my mouth before I can speak.

He moves his hand south, and I break apart from the kiss. That was awful. Instead of tongues dueling in the throes of passion, this was like being orally stabbed by a vengeful dentist.

I grab Bastian's hands as I open my eyes and look at him in the mirror. His eyes are on mine, and he smiles. "Do you like that? Do you like my hands roaming your body?" he asks, trying to continue his journey southward.

I really don't know if I like what's happening right now, but when I'm about to answer him, he distracts me again.

Bastian moves his hands from mine and grabs the bottom of my camisole. I know he wants to pull it off me, but I stop him. My top is midway up when I notice the pendant hanging below, resting just below my breasts.

I freeze when I see the stones and take a quick look at Bastian's eyes. He sees the pendant at the same time, and the weirdest thing happens.

Bastian's eyes flash from bright blue to orange. His irises morph from a perfect circle into long, catlike slits. But it's over, and his eyes are bright blue again. It happens so fast that I don't know if I imagine it or if I really see them change. I move my hand from where I had unknowingly gripped the counter and wrap it around the pendant.

I'm gazing into the depths of the emerald, rotating so I can get a closer view of all the facets. It's almost as if the stone contains a fire.

"I was meaning to ask you if you gave me this. I really don't know where I got this from... well, I don't remember."

"You've always worn that necklace. When I met you, you already had it, and you wear it every day. You told me it was a family heirloom," he tells me while trying to continue with his touch. I keep batting his hand away even though he has me cornered against the sink counter.

"But I don't remember how I got it," I complain.

"Probably because you're still recovering from the accident," Bastian counters.

We are having another mirror stare off when he grabs my hips and turns me around to face him. He doesn't give me a chance to react and kisses me again. This is where the next strangest thing happens. I'm prepared for the onslaught and shut my eyes, trying to savor the moment and reclaim the passion that we seem to have lost.

Yet when I close my eyes and try to return the kiss, I can only see dark eyes, dark wavy hair that still smells like the ocean, and a beautiful smile that doesn't belong to Bastian.

I stop the kiss abruptly and push away from him so I can look at him.

Blond hair, copper highlights, blue eyes, skinny, yet tall, Bastian looks more like a professional runner, not a big city therapist. Bastian drags his hands through his hair, exposing his ears. Pointed.

Fae.

Fuck.

My heart stops, time stops, and everything comes back to me in a blink.

It's so fast that I wince from the pain. I move farther away from Bastian. Holding the counter, I bend over and touch my head, trying to massage out the throb at my temples. It hurts like a motherfucker.

Memory after memory floods my mind. It is so difficult to focus on them. They are clogging up the avenues to my mind. I'm struggling to breathe and stay calm.

Bastian tries to touch my shoulders. At the same time, he asks, "Are you okay, Ana?" I move from his touch, and he flinches.

"DON'T TOUCH ME!" I hiss. I try to stand and look at him. I can't believe this shit right now.

What the fuck is happening? Why am I here? Everything is starting to make sense.

This world. It's a fucking illusion. A damned dream curse. I can't believe I didn't figure it out sooner.

Bastian is the one who cursed me. He's the one who has been trapping me in this dream world. But why? I'm moving my head from side to side, trying to shake out my confusion and blistering headache. I just can't believe this.

"Why?" The question is barely audible, not even a whisper, but it is the only word that my mouth can handle speaking at the moment.

"Why, what? What's wrong? Ana, what's going on with you? You were just fine a couple of minutes ago. Do I need to take you to the doctor?" Bastian tries to come near me with a look of concern written on his face.

But I know better than to believe him. This is all an act. It's fake, and he thinks I don't remember anything. Well, tough shit because I do.

"I. Asked. You. A question." Each word pointed, my voice steadily rises. "Why did you curse me, Bastian? I need an explanation right fucking now!" I'm getting angrier by the second. I can feel a familiar surge of energy inside me. It burns. If he doesn't start talking, I will explode.

"Ana, just… just let me explain please." Bastian moves backward, holding his hands up. His pleading eyes don't have me fooled anymore.

"Well… I'm waiting to know why one of my oldest friends cursed me and then stuck me in a dream where he acted like he was my husband and made me feel like I was going crazy. How did you even create this other world? And why me, Bast? It doesn't make any sense. You know Jace is my mate."

"That's the thing, Ana, you always saw me as a friend, a servant. While I have been living my life thinking of you and wishing that you would see me differently. "When I returned from my studies, I realized that if I wanted to give us our chance for happiness, I didn't have any other choice."

"What do you mean that you didn't have any other choice?"

"Exactly that. You didn't leave me any other choice, Ana. I have done everything in my power to serve you and to make you look at me like a man, not a friend. But you have never given me a chance. I have always just served a purpose to you. I wanted to become your everything, and you never would even accept me as more than a friend.

"The day I came home from medical training, I also found out you were officially bonding to that Water Fae."

Bastian paces the bathroom. When he mentions Jace, disgust crosses his face. Why? What did we do to him? I don't get it. I thought we were all good.

"So I knew I had to act fast. I used the facts I knew about

you to create this other world. I knew that if I wanted to have you, I would need to make sure you had a career that you love and friendship. I scaffolded this dream around you, around your dreams and passions. That was the only way that I could have you. I had to add elements of the truth to the dream so you would latch on to those artifacts and create the rest of the reality. You Ana, you made the dream real for us both.

"And you have been happy here with me. It's the only way I could make our dreams come true, baby. I had to do this. You will understand in time because you don't belong with him, not really, it's me. It should have always been me."

"WHAT the FUCK! It was supposed to be YOU? Was I really happy, Bastian? You fucked with my life." I poke him in the chest.

"And for what? Is my body even here, or is it tucked hidden away unconscious? Were you just going to starve us in this dream world?"

"No, not at all. It's why I would leave so I could check on you and make sure I had sustenance at times…"

"You abandoned me so you could go eat and check on me! Did you even know where I was? That I was going through MY MATING HEAT WITH MY MATE, JACE?

"What… Did that get you off? To know I couldn't control my hormones and would fuck any male that would have me because it's part of a Fae going into heat!

"You made me feel things for you. Things that I thought were real. We had sex!

"Only my MATE has the right to touch my body!

"You… you fucking touched me without my consent! And don't start saying I was willing because I had no idea that I was not in my right mind. How am I going to go home to Jace knowing that I was unfaithful to him?" I'm sobbing, and I start pacing the bathroom. I need to breathe, but it is hard to pull in air.

I start walking to the living room where I start pacing between the couch and the kitchen. Bastian follows me and stands in the corner by the couch. I can't stop my anger. To imagine that all this time, I let him touch me fucks with my head. Jace will be so mad. Oh Jace, my love.

That's when a terrifying thought emerges. Are my babies Bastian's or Jace's? A strangled, inhuman cry leaves my throat.

"FUCK!"

CHAPTER
Twenty~Four

"FUCK!"

I yell at the top of my lungs while grabbing my head. Can I even get pregnant in this fake world? I need to know. I slowly lower myself to my knees and sit back on my heels. "Fuck, fuck, fuck." I keep repeating.

"Ana, calm down baby. There is no need to stress. Jace never has to know. It's simple, Ana. You can stay here with me. We can be happy here and have a life. That's the only thing I want. I want to love you. Please, just let me love you, Ana."

"Ana! My name is not fucking Ana! How dare you call me anything but my full title, I'm Princess Oliviana Chamberlain of the Earth Fae."

"Happiness?" The snarky side of me comes out to play as I continue to rip into Bastian. "How can I be happy here with you? How can you keep me and do this? I don't love you. How did you even curse me? The last time I saw you…"

That's when I realized the moment that it happened. Thank goodness I'm already on the floor, or I may have collapsed. Instead, I angrily point my finger at him.

"You put something in my water on my wedding day.

That's why I started feeling like shit. You grabbed me and put me in that fucking cottage of yours. What was your plan? Huh? Keep me sedated and locked away, in what, YOUR LOVE SHACK?" I'm vibrating with fury.

He grabs his neck with his right hand and looks at me. "Ana... Princess Oliviana..."

"My plan was to take you to a safe place and run with you. I wanted to hide with you and put myself to sleep with the same curse so we could have a life together. It worked to some extent. It would have worked, and you would not know any better. But something failed me, and you kept waking up. When you escaped my home, I followed you, but Jace got to you first.

I followed him to watch how he took you to the cabin. Then I went back to the castle and acted like everything was okay. I could only see you when you were asleep, so I waited for you."

"But there were times when you were not here. Is finding food the only reason that you went away to those supposed conferences?" I say, making quotation marks with my fingers.

"Yeah, but I also had to be in the castle with my dad and keep up the charade that everything was okay. I was trying to find a way to make the curse stronger so we could stay here together forever."

"But what would have happened to our bodies? If we were both asleep, we would have eventually died without food and water."

"My plan was to put us in a stasis where we would not need nutrition. That way, we could still be alive but dreaming. I can still do it. I just need to figure out what went wrong with my magic, I even infused it with my own venom. But now that you know, I want you to stay here with me. I love you, Oliviana... In time, I know you will love me, too." Bastian is practically begging.

I shake my head. I can't believe all this bullshit. He's

fucking crazy. His venom? I didn't think he carried the shifter gene from his mother's side of the family. He's so obsessed with me that he doesn't realize that this is not okay. I never knew he was in love with me. He always acted normal. His dad has been the Supreme Healer in our castle. Bastian grew up learning how to become a healer so he could be the next one when his dad passed away or retired from his position. When I was growing up, he was always there in the castle. We became fast friends when I decided to learn more about our country and the Fae world's customs and culture. I fell in love with reading, and we ended up bonding over our mutual love for books. We would hang out in the library most of the time, and we even hung out with Jace when he came to visit. I thought they were friends.

"Bastian, you know I can't stay here with you. You have always known that I had a fated mate. This is not news to you. Bast, I'm pregnant. Now I'm questioning who is the father of my babies. What am I supposed to do when they're born?" I plead my case to him.

I'm starting to feel some severe anxiety, and I really don't need to have a panic attack right now. I need to find a way to get out of here and break this curse so I can get back to Jace. I bend down and put my head between my knees and try to breathe.

"Ana, calm down. Take deep breaths." Bastian is standing over me, "Are you sure you're pregnant?"

I look up at him. "Yes. I'm pretty positive that I am. I even took a pregnancy test in this dream world, and it was positive. And I met my glows in the Fae Realm."

Bastian sighs. A defeated look crosses his face.

"Your baby is not mine. Everything that we have done in this world is not real. I created this world to have a life where you could fall in love with me. I can't get you pregnant because we are not actually corporeal.

"If the curse is ever broken, everything here will be forgotten. Just like a bad dream, the nightmare will fade away and just leave an uneasiness when you wake up. I want you to understand that I really love you. This dream has been everything that I have ever wanted. I know I went about this the wrong way. I know you are not mine, but I really wanted you to be." Bastian pulls me up and sits us on the couch. "I can't keep you if you are pregnant."

He glances down at my belly. There are a few tears on his cheeks. "I want you, but I will not take their lives away to claim yours."

The sad part about this is that I love him as a friend, but he lost his way. I need to make sure that he tells me how to break this curse. I need to stay nice. I don't know what would happen if I start screaming at him. That's what I really want to do. I want to use my power to bury him and leave him to rot on the dirt.

Bastian wipes his tears and looks at me.

"What went wrong with the curse? You almost got me believing that this is the real world and that I was going crazy," I tell him.

"Well, I tried to spell your necklace, but it didn't work the way it was supposed to. Apparently, the power of that pendant is too strong and fights the curse. I knew that it needed to be something you always wear. I just didn't count on the mating bond. It is too strong for me, and since the pendant holds both halves of your soul, the magic of the curse and powers are in constant conflict. That's why you would oscillate between worlds every time you fell asleep. It's why I made up the accident to explain why you would drift between worlds, so you would think the real world is just a made-up fantasy, a forgotten dream."

Now I'm beginning to understand. The fire in the cabin, how the pendant got warm every time I touched it. How it always caught my eye. It was like the pendant wanted me to know about the curse. What if the pendant is the key to breaking this curse? It has to be. If I keep asking questions, he'll know I'll do something to stop him. I need to tread carefully.

"We need to go back, Bastian. You just can't keep me here. Now that I know what's really happening, I won't stay here. We need to go back now."

Bastian shakes his head. His nostrils flare. I can see his earlier resolution to let me go dissolve right in front of me as he grabs my upper arms tightly.

"No, not Ana. I will make the curse stronger. I can make this work, even with the babies. I will make you fall in love with me again, and we will be happy. I can put them into stasis, too, and they will be ours. Forever our babies. They never have to grow up. They can stay small, and we can take care of them always."

This man has lost his fucking mind. He pretended to let me leave but changed his mind as soon as he had a new idea for keeping me.

I won't let him do that to me. I must stay calm.

Bending my head, I reach for my powers. They're faint, but they are there. Just buried under his spell.

Too bad I'm stronger, and nothing can be buried from an Earth Fae. Burrowing is my thing, as long as I can avoid worms. They are seriously yucky, beneficial, yes, but also gross.

I think about Jace and our life together. All of the good memories I have about us and the memories I want to create with our babies. The pendant gets warm, the heat permeating through my breasts into my heart.

I can feel Jace's and my combined powers. They are getting stronger by the second. What can I do with all this power? I feel so full of energy that I can almost explode with untamed energy.

Focusing it all on the pendant, I unclasp the stone from the chain. As I hold it in my hands, the opal vibrates in its copper cage.

I take a moment to look up at Bastian, who is starting to panic.

"Ana, what are you doing?" He stands from the couch and starts walking away from me. "Princess Oliviana... I don't think you understand what you are..."

I stand, and using all the power coursing through my body, I extend my right hand, holding the pendant in front of me. "Simple, I'm stopping you. I'm *not* going to be stuck here with you."

"Ana, baby, please. Stay with me. I can make all our dreams come true."

"Our dreams, or do you mean your dreams? They are not my dreams, Bastian. We don't want the same thing, and we never have." I keep him talking at the same time as I focus on my next step. I'm letting my Earth and Water magic guide me. I really don't know what I'm doing, but I have this strong feeling. It's like they're leading me to do what needs to be done.

I hear Jace's voice in the back of my mind. Something he said at The Fabricate. What was it? A thought surfaces. Yes, that's it. I remember now. I grab the memory and hold on tight.

"Once forged together, the stones cannot be undone. Cataclysmic events would occur if they were to break as the stones fight to merge back together. This is a permanent weld of two very strong forces, Earth and Water. Once combined, it's forever, Livi. Do you understand? Once we forge this pendant, it will harness our powers. Our mating bond establishes the connection, and it cannot be separated. We cannot control what would happen if this occurs. Remember this, my love." I remember... Jace was telling me the cons of forging our powers together using the anvil. It was risky, but now I realize the importance and necessity of our

choice. He was making sure I understood there would be consequences if…

I know what to do now. I look at the pendant in my hand. Bastian is just a blur in the background as I focus on the junction of the emerald, pearl, and copper. The barest flicker of power bends, doing my request, releasing the delicate weld.

I'm still holding the pendant when suddenly, the pendant breaks, splitting into three pieces, black pearl spinning and hovering in the air, the emerald, which is now engulfed in flames, and the copper wire, which floats suspended between the two stones. A large booming sound follows as a bright light floods the room. My eyes hurt from the intense brightness. Green flares of light escape the emerald as the pearl begins to dance around the stone. Faster and faster, the pearl's orbit grows closer and closer to the emerald. The copper wire is electrified, pulsing with magnetism as it, too, is drawn toward the emerald. Lightning discharges from the wire as it bends and begins to rewrap around the pearl. The momentum of the pearl accelerates, and the sphere enlarges, growing in size as the emerald pulls it closer.

When they connect, another loud *BANG* occurs as they merge. Just like two hydrogen atoms forming the essence of stars, the collision is massive and unstable. The pendant goes supernova and erupts. The energy rushes outward, moving beyond this room. Then just as quickly as it left, the power gets sucked back in. I can feel the charge of the energy as it returns. All of the magic focuses where the pendant spins together once more.

The stones glow brighter, blinding. I can't see, but I can feel the heat and the combination of forces.

I close my eyes and feel a bigger rush of energy. Then nothing. The world goes quiet. I open my eyes. Floating in front of me is a very small but very bright and shiny white speck, a singularity is pulsing rhythmically. The stillness, the silence is fleeting. Before I can blink, the energy collapses inward on itself, birthing a swirling vortex of darkness.

Oh fuck, I think. *This is not good.*

I move backward as fast as I can, hitting a wall.

I look over to the side. Bastian is being pulled toward the black hole. He looks at me with panicked eyes. "What have you done? Don't do this to me, Ana," Bastian yells at me while he's being sucked closer to the black hole.

I stand there in shock because I don't know what happened or how I made it happen. I gain a moment of clarity and lunge, trying to catch Bastian before he's pulled away from me. I know what he did isn't right, but I can't just let him die. I'm better than that.

I grab his hands and yell, "Hold on!"

The vortex is growing in size, and energy whips around the room, blowing everything around. It sounds like we are in the middle of a tornado.

Bastian's fingers start to slip from mine as I try to back up toward the front door. If I can just get us through the door, maybe we'll have a chance to escape.

But the gravity from the swirling void is too much. One by one, I lose my grip.

"ANA!" Bastian screams as he slips away.

"BASTIAN!"

Then he's gone. Just gone.

But the vortex is still there, and it's growing, and it seems angrier.

CHAPTER
Twenty~Five

POOF!

Nothing. It's only me in the living room now.

Bastian is gone.

Just like that, poof. My heart drops. I didn't love Bastian, but I didn't want this. There is due process, an order of events that must occur for redemption. Maybe it's my willful heart, or perhaps I'm too kind or too nice, but I truly believe everyone can find deliverance. Gain redemption from misdeeds and crimes. My mom once told me that I have the "Savior" syndrome. She says "Savior" was a fable about a little faeling who had all sorts of wicked things done to them. And even though the girl dies at the end of the story, she always held strongly onto one belief, that deep down inside, everyone has goodness. It's all about finding it. Sometimes it takes a deeper investigation. Or maybe just a bit of tenacity and persistence. Who knows, maybe that's for another story to be delivered on a different date.

The sounds of picture frames and light fixtures being ripped from the walls and ceiling bring me back to my current reality. That Bastian really is gone.

And... so is everything else in this house, this world. One by one, item after item gets sucked into the vortex of the void.

Oh fuck. Now, how am I going to get back to my world?

I make my way to the front door as I navigate picture frames and random knickknacks that dangerously whirl into the rapidly accelerating vortex. But when I engage the handle, it's locked. Fear courses down my spine. I reach for the latch, yet it's not there, either. My breath catches. I cannot unlock this door. Anxiety ricochets through me, head to toe. I clench my fists. There must be another way back home.

"Oliviana Chamberlain. You are not going down like this," I tell myself, grounding my feet in the fact that I will make it back to Jace and our families. "You are a strong Earth Fae mated to an amazing Water Fae. You are about to be a mother. You will survive." I chant this mantra over and over, building confidence as I strategize.

This is a dream world, so it doesn't exist. How did I get here? Well, that was easy enough to answer. When I go to sleep something happens and I switch worlds. How do I normally leave here? Again, when I go to sleep in this dream, I wake up in another reality. It seems simple enough. I just need to go back to sleep, and I should wake up back home in the Fae world.

I just need to go to sleep, with an angry vortex ripping this nightmarishly blanch home to shreds. Great. Just wonderful. *Positive, Livs, stay positive,* I tell myself.

But how am I supposed to lie down and sleep with an void vortex that is slowly growing more enraged and larger as it absorbs everything into oblivion?

Bump that. Where am I supposed to go lie down and just sleep?

I look around. The vortex is on the other side of the house from a guest room. There, I hope it has a bed.

I skirt around the edge of the room and slip inside the guest room. It's white, obviously, Bastian had no color vision when he created this world. But it will do. I climb on the bed and crawl under the covers. At least this way if it doesn't work, I can pretend to be hiding if the black hole succeeds in sucking me away.

I'm shaking. How do I do this? I took Benadryl once before, but that was in the master bedroom. I can do that again. If this is a dream, nothing will happen to my babies. I start to cry. *Oh, my babies. They don't deserve this.* Between sobs, I hold on to the sheets, wishing. This was a bad move. I shouldn't have come in here. I need to move and fast. Time is running out as the door starts to rattle and shake off its hinges.

Taking a risk, I get out of the guest bed and throw open the door just in time for the vortex to suck it away and run as fast as I can to the master bedroom. I don't even look in the direction of the vortex as I hurry. I can hear it, though, furious energy as it drags in piece by piece of this world. I make it to the en suite bathroom and grab the bottle of Benadryl from the cabinet. Last time I took three pills, so I'm going to do the same thing, that way I know I will wake up… Hopefully in the Fae world.

I sit back on my bed, drink the pills, and wait for the medicine to take effect, wanting to get as comfortable as possible while trying not to panic. I really need this to work, and I'm terrified about how this decision will impact my babies.

Once more, I hear Jace in the back of my mind, whispering. "Oliviana… Livi… morning glory. My mate, come home to me."

I force my body to relax and bring my mind into a meditative trance.

I fade, I drift. Finally, I sleep.

Just as the master bedroom succumbs to the vortex's infuriatingly relentless pull and this reality is ripped away.

CHAPTER
Twenty-Six

I WAKE UP SLOWLY. My joints ache, my muscles are stiff, and the chill of a cool surface penetrates my bones.

Gathering my bearings as I sit up, I first realize I'm not in a bed but on the cold, hard linoleum floor of an examination room. I'm somehow located in the castle mortuary. The second thing I realize, the worst part, is not remembering a damn thing about how I got here and why I'm lying on the floor. The last thing I remember was the Supreme Healer escorting Jace and me to the… Where were we going? I shake the fog out of my head.

Right, we were going to check out our babies. We needed the potions in his clinic so he could cast an image.

I take a moment to rise, holding on to a metal frame to help me get up. I brush myself off as I stand. I'm not next to a frame or a shelf and realize I'm using an old iron gurney to catch my balance. I quickly let go and step away. Iron… If I was there, then how did I fall? And what about my powers? I hold my palm out and open, letting both Earth and Water magic form an interconnected lattice that vines around my arm. I hold the magic in place as I observe the other object in the room.

There is a second gurney next to the one I touched, but I don't see anyone else here. Instead, there is a leather-bound book with a large clasp locking the book together. I walk around and pick up the book. There is no key nor an owner to help explain how to open the lock. Who put it here? Why? I tuck the book into my dress pockets. This will require further investigation as soon as I remember why in the world I came here.

A faint flutter comes from my navel, like a little kick from the inside. Two glows appear in my mind, bouncing impatiently.

Oh goddesses, Jace. I remember! He's not here. I turn around to leave but wobble a little before I regain my balance. My legs are still stiff from being on the cold floor.

I take off toward the room where we saw our children. Arriving quickly, I fling open the doors. No one is in the waiting area. No Jace. I run into the back hallways, heading toward the only other place he would be, Dr. Baron's personal exam room.

I pause at the entrance, two curtains wide-open, revealing the room where I first saw my twins.

Jace lies near the bed on the floor facing the entrance, but his eyes are closed. My mom and Milly are both slumped nearby next to him—Milly propped up near a chair and Mom sprawled out on the floor, her golden hair spread around her like a fading sunrise over the ocean. The two appear to be asleep.

I rush over to Jace and shake him. There is no response. I feel for his pulse and relax when I finally detect a steady heartbeat. Mom and Milly are the same.

It's as if they are all asleep. But what if they're dead? At least they're breathing. What happened?

My heart feels like it's going to beat out of my chest. I make another round, checking over each person I love. This doesn't make any sense. Where is the Supreme Healer? Did something bad happen to him?

A groan from behind the curtain catches my attention. I move over and pull it to the side. Dr. Baron lies on his stomach, one of his strange machines on top of him. I use my magical energy to lift the device off his body and set it to the side. Then I go to the healer.

He, too, is mostly asleep. But there are small signs that he's stirring and waking up. I roll him to his back and grab a lab coat to put under his head.

Dr. Baron, my mother, and Milly are starting to move and wake up... except Jace. I use my magic to lift Jace to the bed I occupied while Dr. Baron examined the babies. I brush my fingers through his hair. I crawl into the bed and cradle his head in my lap. Gently, I rock us. I lean my forehead to Jace's and close my eyes. "Jace, wake up, my love." I place kisses on his face, but he doesn't move. I look up and see Mom and Milly are now wide awake, sitting on the floor.

"What happened?" asks Milly. "I feel like I'm hungover from too much wine. Why were we day drinking, Mama Queenie? Livs, you weren't drinking, were you? I sure hope not."

"Milly, hush," my mom scolds. "What happened, Oliviana? Where is Dr. Baron? What's wrong with Jace?" My mom is asking too many questions that I cannot answer.

One question answers itself for me. Dr. Baron groans again before letting us all know, "Here, I'm here. Is everyone okay? What happened?"

"I don't know. I woke up on the floor of the mortuary wing and was alone. I started looking for Jace when I found all of you here, asleep. Now you are all awake. Well, everyone except Jace. And I don't know about Dad either. I haven't left this room since I found the three of you."

I'm gazing down at my mate, tears filling my eyes. I brush the back of my hand across my cheeks.

"Jace... sweetheart, my lighthouse. Please come back to me, come home to me." I press a kiss to his lips.

My heart is hurting. I start to move my lips from Jace's when I hear a low growl before hands are tangling themselves in my hair. Jace pulls me closer, deepening our kiss. I try to pull away, but he refuses to let me go. So I give in and kiss my mate with everything I have in me.

Eventually, he lets me go. I look into his dark onyx eyes and see my reflection staring back at me. My hair is a big fuzzy mess from where he pulled my hair during our kiss, or maybe it was already a nightmare from earlier.

"Jace." I start, but I have no words.

"Livi," he says as he slowly sits up. He turns in the hospital bed to face me. "What was that for? What happened? Why am I in bed with you? Livi love, why are you crying?"

Tears cascade freely as I grab Jace's face and pepper it with kisses.

When I'm done, I take a moment to explain everything to Jace. I can tell he's getting upset, but he holds his anger, holding me close and pressing his own kisses into my hair and on my forehead.

Dr. Baron clears his throat, "Uh, Your Highnesses, Majesty, Miss Mildred, if I may suggest... should we, uh... I mean... shouldn't we go find the king?"

———

We get to the doors of my father's office and see them slightly cracked open.

My father never leaves the doors open, whether he's in there or not. Those gates are shut.

"Oh no!" my mother exclaims.

Jace pushes the doors open the rest of the way, allowing light from the hallway to flood the darkened room. I cannot see much but make out a shape slumped near the desk.

Rubbing my hands together, I gather my Earth magic, creating friction. Using the fluidity that Jace gives me from his Water magic, I produce a glowing blue orb that lights up the entire room.

Hunched over on the floor beside his desk, my dad, too, looks asleep. My mother runs over to him, wailing.

Milly, Jace, and I rush over, but Dr. Baron halts us. "Your Majesties! Please stop and let me examine the king before you destroy or contaminate any evidence. Your Highness, Queen Lydia, please, let me do my job and check on your husband."

We watch as Dr. Baron bends over to check his pulse. He looks back and nods.

I walk around to the backside of my father's desk. He has a panic switch that sends a signal to the royal guards. It was installed if we ever had to evacuate and hide in this room, but now I'm more than grateful for my father's random paranoia. I flip the switch and walk back over to Jace. He wraps me in his arms, cradling my head against his chest. We can't do anything now but wait.

It doesn't take long. In less than a minute, the royal guards rush into my father's office, weapons raised and ready to protect my family.

However, my father is already stirring. The telltale signs of King Oryon waking up as he growls and stretches out, elongating his body as his joints pop. The sounds reverberate through the room. They mimic the cracking of the Earth and the fast flow of wind through the trees.

The guards look around, slightly confused since no active, visible threat is attacking anyone. Just my dad, loudly waking up.

"Dr. Baron, Lydia, kids, what's going on?" my dad inquires as he finally opens his eyes and sits up.

"Well, Dad... I called for the guards because you were passed out when we came in here. However, you were already waking up when they arrived."

"Asleep? I wasn't asleep. I just finished sending a transmission to the chef to discuss dinner." My dad addresses me before he turns to talk to Dr. Baron. "Your son stopped by to let me know you all would be in the clinic longer than expected. I didn't know he was back from university. You must be awfully proud," my dad says to the doctor.

"The point is, I told him that was fine and asked him to deliver a message. I just can't remember what I asked him to tell you all. Besides, where did the lad get off to? Have you seen your boy yet? Maybe he already told you what I forgot."

My dad taps his head. "Old age, you know, gets to the mind these days."

"No, I haven't seen Bastian since he left home this morning. It's not my job to keep tabs on that boy. He probably got lost in some daydream somewhere," Dr. Baron replies to my dad.

"Your Highness, sir," a guard interrupts. "Did you need us or...?"

"Well, since you're here, yes. Do a perimeter check, make all the precautionary measures, and ask the night guards to double their watch efforts. Report back to me every hour. I would rather be safe and proactive. But I think the rest of us are good. Let's go eat and celebrate the creation of my grandchildren!"

I look up at Jace. He bends down, placing a kiss on my lips. "Come on, my morning glory, let's go feed that impatient, hangry father of yours."

We follow hand-in-hand behind my parents. Milly grabs my other hand, swinging my arm back and forth.

Walking to dinner, I think about how fortunate I am for my family and the babies coming soon. I can't wait to meet them and complete this dream come true.

CHAPTER
Twenty~Seven
SIX MONTHS LATER

THE FLUTTER of movement in my belly catches my attention.

"Jace." I gasp as I grab his hand and put his palm on my belly. Twin flutters kick at his fingers.

We smile. Jace holds me as we gaze into the woods outside our cabin. We look into the forest for a few more moments before Jace says, "Come on, morning glory, time to go to bed."

He guides me back inside with his hand on my lower back. Shutting the door behind us, I turn into his arms and give him a long, slow kiss. He returns the kiss just as deeply. Leaning into his arms, I sigh. "I love you, Jace Seaborne."

"I love you, too, Oliviana Chamberlain Seaborne. Now, let's get some sleep so we can wake up and make all our dreams really come true."

Oh, I love how that sounds. Oliviana Chamberlain Seaborn. I officially became his wife a couple of weeks after I found everyone asleep at the castle. This ceremony was simpler than the first one.

We still don't know what happened to me at our first wedding. Apparently, I was found in the woods knocked out. Nobody knows how I got there, but Jace found me and took me to our cabin, where we spent our mating moon together. That's when I got pregnant with the twins.

After a few weeks, Jace got concerned because I slept a lot and ran high fevers. So he decided to take me back to the castle to be checked by the Supreme Healer. There, we all passed out. I woke up first, followed by the rest of my family.

We never figured out why we were all asleep or why I ended up in the mortuary. Dr. Baron thinks it was some random fluke or power flux. The search is still ongoing for this mysterious phenomenon.

We also have an open investigation into Dr. Baron's son, Bastian. He disappeared the same day and hasn't been seen since. It's been six months since his disappearance. His family is concerned, but he didn't leave any indication that he was going. My father has sent messages to all the other kingdoms to see if he's there, but so far, no one knows where he is. Everyone has a theory. Some say that he moved to another kingdom, others say he was in love with someone and he ran off with her, and others think that he died somewhere in the woods and has not been found. The *Fae Tributary* has been covering his case, but there have been no new reports in months. Recently, Milly told me that one of our younger classmates at the academy is now a new reporter and had recently begun digging through the pieces. I even gave Milly the leather bound journal I found to pass on to Vesper, hoping it helps her solve the puzzle.

The reality is that we don't know. Everyone is sad and misses him. He was a good friend to us, and I hope that wherever he's at, he's happy.

Back to reminiscing about our wedding, I allow my thoughts to be swept toward our matrimonial festivities.

Jace and I decided to have a small ceremony in his kingdom, Quartzside.

I wanted a beach wedding, and my mate did not disappoint. We went to his family's castle and started planning a very intimate wedding. Jace's mom and my mom were so excited that they took over all the planning, with Milly filling in the gaps. We only invited our family, which turned out to still be quite a few Fae since we all have multiple siblings, except for me, I just have my older brother Lucas. We live in a fertile time with families often having several sets of twins and triplets.

Since the wedding was smallish, my mom had the great idea of inviting reporters from all four kingdoms so they could write about the wedding and share it with the world. Especially since the first wedding was an epic disaster. Luckily, the public just attributes the Fae mating heat to me becoming a runaway bride.

Being a writer in the Fae world is extremely important because Fae Authors are in charge of sharing news, letters, and other information that is later used and modified to become books. The manuscripts are filled with our story so the next generation can be informed of all the important events.

Besides, it wasn't every day that a prince and princess would get married a second time, so this was big news.

The ceremony took place on the beach near Jace's parents' castle. The beach had powdery white sand that extended for more than five miles. Crystal clear and azure waters were a sight to be seen, stretching past the horizon.

Birds coasted through the gentle waves, dipping their wings into the surf as they hunted the shining fish below the surface.

One of the things that I love the most about the beaches in this kingdom is that during the nighttime, you can see the dark blue and silver fishes swimming, glowing luminescence pouring from them as they move around in the water. There are other protozoans that have biofluorescence lighting up the path as you glide through the water.

We were married on a jetty created just for us. It was wide

enough to place a few rows of chairs along the edges. At the end of the jetty, my mom created a beautiful arch of colorful flowers representing the wild flora found in both the forest and the ocean. Red roses twined between yellow tulips. Bright pink hibiscus set heavy with creamy oak leaf hydrangeas. Even tiny blue forget-me-knots were sewn into the pattern.

For our second attempt, I wore a simple light-blue dress made of light tulle and silk instead of my green gown. The bodice was covered in pastel rhinestones and fitted perfectly to my curves. I created a beautiful crown of seashells and flowers I found on a walk that morning. I let my hair cascade down my back with loose beach waves. I chose to skip the shoes, walking to my mate barefoot, one with the Earth and Ocean.

Jace wore beautiful dark blue trousers and a light-blue shirt combination. He looked so handsome that day. His shirt was open, exposing the ridge of his collarbone where it dips down toward his muscled chest.

I walked down the aisle with my dad beside me. He cried the entire time.

When the ceremony was over, the flowers on the arch started losing petals, flying, swirling around us. All the Earth Fae present caused more petals and shells to fly around us as we returned to the tent set at the beach near the jetty. Ocean Fae cast misty bubbles, floating them in and out of the twirling flowers and shells. Inside the tent were a few tables where our guests sat to eat and celebrate with us. At the end of the night, my feet hurt from all the dancing. As Jace carried me bridal style to our honeymoon suite, I used the moment to place open-mouth kisses along his exposed skin, slowly unbuttoning the rest of his shirt as I continued my tormenting tease. What can I say? It was the best night of my life. We made it to the beach in front of our seaside villa before Jace lost control and ravaged my body in the best ways.

————

Two years later

"Jace," I yell.

I need my husband to come and help me with these kids. Who would have thought that having twins would be so difficult? They will be two years old soon, and if this is how they are now, I don't want to imagine how they will be when they're teenagers.

Jonah is a very sweet boy. He looks just like his dad, with dark hair and eyes. He's always helping his sister. Even though they are so little, he always makes sure she's okay. Jonah was born two minutes after Oleana but has always acted as the older brother.

On the other hand, Lea, as I love to call her, is terrible. She's identical to Jonah, but her eyes are bright green like mine, with a hint of blue streaking through the irises. My darling Oleana looks like a sweet child, but let me tell you, that girl doesn't listen to me. The worst part is that Jace is putty in her hands. She can do anything, and with one smile or a tear, she has her dad eating from the palm of her hands. The other day, I was out with Milly when Lea just took off her clothes because they hurt.

Meanwhile back here in the living area, Jonah is trying to help me keep her clothes on, but we cannot keep her decent nor make that girl happy. Needless to say, she's a handful, but I love her and Jonah with all my heart. They make our family complete.

Jace wants to have more kids, but I think I want to wait a little bit before I start thinking about having more. I have my hands full with these two that are currently filled with mud around them. Since they discovered they had powers, they've used them against each other all the time.

Oleana likes to throw water at her brother, and Jonah likes

to respond by throwing dirt, making a mess everywhere they are. Sounds familiar.

"What's wrong, my morning glory?" Jace enters the living room, and suddenly stops when he sees the mess on the floor and the kids covered in mud. "Again? Really?"

He walks toward the kids while I tell him, "I told you to stop teaching Lea how to use her water powers. She's always fighting with Jonah and ends up throwing water all over him."

Jace looks at me and smiles sheepishly. He knows I'm right, but he doesn't care. He reaches the kids and grabs Jonah from the floor and holds him away from his chest so he doesn't get mud on his clothes.

"Daddy," says Jonah, trying to get closer to Jace. But Oleana starts crying when she sees that her dad has her brother in his arms and not her. I go to grab Oleana from the floor, but she doesn't want me to. She sends a ball of water my way, and I swipe my hand to the side so it lands beside me.

"Oleana, stop with the water right now!" I say in my mommy's voice. She ignores me and starts crying harder for her dad. I look at Jace, and he sighs. He ends up putting Jonah on his chest and bending down to pick up Olena as well. She stops crying all of a sudden and smiles at Jace.

She reaches her dirty hand toward his cheek. "Daddy, I wove you," she says to him and leans to kiss him.

"I love you more, my beautiful girl, my wild rose." He smiles and takes off with them to the bathroom to get washed up for dinner while I clean the mess in the living room.

I can hear Lea telling Jace about her and Jonah's day as he turns on the water to the tub. I can imagine her dumping extra bubble soap as she excitedly explains to her father, hands moving wildly as she says in her baby voice, "Daddy, Jonah and I caught a butterfly today! It was bright green and..."

"Oleana, that's enough bubbles! You and Jonah will float away just like those butterflies if you make too many." I hear Jace tease.

Smiling, I wave a hand to clean up the muddy mess before walking over to the doorway and watching my family. Jonah is already in the tub. I'm pretty sure he still has his shoes on, and Jace is trying to wrangle the bubble soap from Lea. This life is definitely my reality, and I'm so happy it's mine.

———

Later, when the kids are asleep in their room, Jace and I lie in bed after having amazing sex. My head is on his chest while he is still seated deep with me. We are both breathing hard and a little sweaty.

"I love you, Oliviana, and I want you to know that you made my dreams come true."

"I love you, too, my mate, my Jace."

I kiss his chest and close my eyes, thinking our dreams really had come true.

Epilogue

BASTIAN

WELL... I fucked that up. I mean really, deeply fucked up.

That didn't go according to plan at all. What the fuck was I thinking?

Kidnap Princess Oliviana and curse her into a dream world?

Yup. I fucked up.

And now here I am, floating around in this unavoidable abyss. My snake is itching to be released and stretched out. How nice it would be to bask in a sunray while I watch the Chamberlains and Seabornes go about their daily lives.

Sure. I could explain my reasons for mentally kidnapping the princess, but there are no excuses. I wanted her. It was simple, really. Plain, lust-filled want. I had hoped to keep her, to treasure her. But no.

The reptile in me saw her as a sparkling prize, a trophy to covet.

Yet the mate bond was too powerful to keep her asleep, even with my own venom injected into the potion, and in a safe place, where I could watch after her. I had watched after Ana for her entire life, nurtured her health, and saw her grow up into the most beautiful woman. Sigh. Not my woman. No.

She may have been the woman who I wanted to ensnare in my heart, but she's the woman who trapped me in this endless dark plane. I wish there was a do-over. I'm just so… sooo.

Fucked.

I'm so fucking lonely. I don't remember when I came here or how long I've been floating.

I'm trying to decide what's worse: the endless dark, the unavoidable floating, or the inability to feel, to touch, to just have a conversation with another person. What I would give to just talk to someone, anyone.

Would anyone even listen after what I have done? I know I wouldn't. I can't even feel the pain from my despair. Fuck! I want to cry, but I no longer have form.

If I could just scratch that itch under that one scale…

Yeah, to say I fucked up is nice. That fucking supernova was kinder than my actions. I know I deserve this.

Yet I wish…

I wish for that sunshine, to feel it on my face, even if it burns. To feel the wind blowing through my hair, even if it carries me away. Begrudgingly, I admit to myself I want to feel the same love that radiates from my Ana and her Jace. But who would ever love a serpent hybrid whose only Earth Fae powers reside in understanding the layers of dirt I can burrow through? I'm no better than a worm. My own mother birthed me and took off, leaving me with a jealous asshole of a father.

If only someone were ferocious enough to see me as their challenge, to truly see me, the man. Not the broken halfling whose publicly respected father beats and shreds my being every evening behind closed doors. If only someone knew my story. If they only understood, if they cared about an Earth Fae whose deepest, darkest secret is also being a snake shifter. A hybrid, a misfit, forged because one snake shifting mother went into heat at the same time she slithered into a possessive, domineering Earth Fae who claimed her as his. Too bad she only stuck around long enough to birth my brothers and me before she wriggled out of his grasp and escaped.

The only thing I can do as I float is to ruminate and dream. It's these dreams, these wishes that become my infinite reality. I dream of deliverance, a delusion I hold in hopes someone will discover me and love me.

AND SUBSCRIBE

IF YOU WANT to know more about Oliviana and Jace signup for our Newsletter to receive the Extended Epilogue. Find us on Social Media and send us a picture of the book so we can send you the link for the extended epilogue

———

To know more about our next book follow us on Social Media and Subscribe to our Newsletter.

You can also join our Facebook SweetTart Group.

Social Media Handle: @mariatandyauthor

Acknowledgments

María

I want to start by thanking Tandy, without you I would have not been able to write a book. I have always loved to read and I started to want to write my own stories but I was afraid of writing in English, but with you by my side I made my dream of becoming an author come true. I LOVE YOU GIRL!

I also want to thank my husband and kids that let me work on this project and let me be for a few hours a day so I can finish my writing. Esteban eres el mejor esposo del mundo GRACIAS por todo el amor y apoyo que siempre me has brindado.

Mom, you were the first person I told that I was writing this book. I explained all the plot to you and you loved it. Gracias Mami porque sin ti no sería la persona que soy. TE AMO MUCHO. Thanks to my niece Emily and sister Janet, for your input on this story and all the love that I have receive from you guys!

Thanks to our girlfriends Andrea, Sabrina and Angela. You guys put up with us at work and helped us develop this story to make it a reality. We LOVE you girls. Andrea I hope you love our trashy novel, we wrote the sex scenes JUST for you :)

I also want to thank Eunice for making this amazing cover and for being part of this new journey. Eva, thanks for being supportive and lastly to Melissa, thank you so much for you valuable input. Without it this story would not be completed.

Tandy

I want to take a moment and thank María. I was blessed five years ago when you moved into the classroom across the hallway. Three years ago we both realized our shared love for raunchy romance novels. Especially those that had a bit of fantasy embedded in the story. Two years ago we both expressed our desire to write our own naughty story that combined our Puerto Rican, Russian, and American heritages. That first story is still in the works and who knows, maybe one day we will finish and publish that manuscript, too. Then, one random night Spring 2023 I had a really weird dream that felt was too real, too confusing. I told you about the dream and how it could be an idea for a book. You jumped on the **Delusional Dreams** bandwagon and here we are, several months later, we have our first actual novel!!!! It has been an incredible journey getting to write, giggle, and imagine with you. I still cannot believe we actually wrote the sex scenes. I am turning red just thinking about them. Anywho, I love you lady and I am so grateful you are on this adventure with me.

To our friends, especially the women in our lives, thank you for being our moms, sisters, cousins, aunts, besties, soul-mates. Your encouragement has energized our creativity and ambition. To the moments we stole for ourselves to write, thank you for giving us the time to outline, organize, and edit.

To our husbands, yeah we wrote about sex, don't worry, we still only flick our beans to you. And maybe our book boyfriends because we designed them after you two. ;) Я тебя очень люблю.

To Tulip, Fiona, and Basil, thank you for being my foot napping furries and staying up late with me while I wrote and imagined life in the Fae World.

María & Tandy

To our education family. We could not have pursued this dream without your love, support, and never ending laughs. Life truly blessed us when we found ourselves in classrooms across the hallway from each other and with you all in our lives.

Last but not less important, we want to thank you, our Dear Reader for picking up this book and giving us a chance. We hope you love this book and we would like to hear from you!

About

THE AUTHORS

MARÍA TANDY ARE two teacher friends that one day decided to chase their dreams and write novels together. Across the hall from each other, María and Tandy use their creative energy to inspire their students as well as cultivate a welcoming atmosphere at their school filled with love and laughter.

María is a sassy Puertorrican that loves romance and

enjoys reading in her free time. María is a Spanish teacher by day and a writer by night. She has a fantastic husband that is better than any book boyfriend and three amazing kids.

Tandy is a saucy Alabama girl who loves all things science in the writing duo. When not in her STEM classroom you can find Tandy in one of her many gardens, kayaking a creek, spoiling her fur-babies, working on her research, or curled up next to her husband reading while listening to vinyl.

Made in the USA
Columbia, SC
12 October 2024

43472791R00133